Taylor Caldwell

WICKED
ANGEL

FAWCETT PUBLICATIONS, INC., GREENWICH, CONN.
MEMBER OF AMERICAN BOOK PUBLISHERS COUNCIL, INC.

A CREST
REPRINT

In the
spine-chilling tradition of
THE BAD SEED,
Taylor Caldwell
weaves a horror-rimmed portrait.
It is a picture you will not easily forget.

"The wicked ones, who are constantly being born amongst us, are often distinguished by appearing as angels of light and wit and intelligence, charming and fascinating beyond usual mortal endowments, apparently loving and always exciting love even among those who are of a usually cynical nature. In truth, they appear most lovable and amiable, for it is their diabolical genius to be all things to all men, grave among the grave, gay among the gay, sympathetic in the company of those of sensibility, never openly hostile or belligerent; flexible of temperament, of an open countenance and invariably possessed of great magnetism. —More of these wicked ones are born in each generation than we know of, but those who are unfortunately of their blood know that they entertain a demon, and not unawares. May God preserve you and me from encountering one such in marriage or among our children!"

—Proust

CHAPTER ONE

He could feel the rage suddenly flaring in him. He liked to feel rage, for it meant not only a quick warm flooding about his loins, a hot, watery flooding, but also an intense inner excitement that made him experience a voluptuous heightening of all sensation. The external flooding brought his mother, full of coos and murmurs and exclamations meant to be chiding but which were really endearing, giving him new importance. Unless, of course, SHE was there, as SHE was today, SHE, the deeply knowing, the deeply hated. On the few occasions when he had been alone with HER, and SHE had angered him and so induced him to let out the flood, there had been no cooings, no pretended scoldings which were later compensated for with candies and cookies; there had been only a harsh smiting on his buttocks, disgusted huge eyes glaring at him, words of contempt, and then the pushing away into a solitary room. He had never forgotten or forgiven. He hated HER; he would always hate HER. He dared not let loose the flood today; he dared not experiment to see if Mum would protect him from another assault, another stare of repulsion, more words of contempt. He was very sensitive, as were all his kind. He understood, at four years, without words.

No, he must hold back the flood which welled in him with his rage; his face wrinkled with emotion and hate and self-pity. He wailed very softly as he sat on the doorstep outside the kitchen door.

The voices went on, the voice of Mum and the voice of the hated HER, and he could understand very little. He glowered. A pretty beetle ran near his foot and he crushed it and smiled. He rubbed the innocent slime into the concrete with his heel. A butterfly flew close to him, and

7

he darted out his hand to destroy it; it was very lovely, but also wary. It blew away from him, and he shrilled indignantly, and rubbed his buttocks on the step. The garden, in full hot summer, lay all about him, golden, rose, white, violet, red, blue, and the maple trees held their fretted green banners to the shining sky. The grass glittered in the sun; the birds bustled on it, and, chattering, rose into the trees, or sat at a distance on the old gray stone wall. He looked at it all restlessly; he leaned over and tore up a clump of grass at the side of the concrete walk, and amused himself by ripping apart each blade separately. He kicked the stuffed bear below him. He put his thumb into his mouth again, and again whined, and looked at the birds and hated them, and hated the voices in the kitchen behind him. For now he understood that they were no longer discussing him, and this was outrageous. For there was nothing in the world as valuable and as precious as himself; nothing significant lived in the world besides him, and the world was made to serve him, to wait upon his smiles, to stand beside his bed, to put delicious morsels into his mouth, to amuse him, to cry and laugh over him, to clap hands delightedly at his exploits, to turn in his direction adoring faces and worn, worshiping simpers. Dimly, as he tore viciously at the grass, he was tearing viciously at HER, and destroying HER, who dared not to bend with supple waist and knee before him, and acknowledge him for the mighty creature he was.

Kathy Saint, who preferred to be known as Katherine, delicately tasted the chicken broth she was preparing for her son. The fine skin between her eyes puckered, and she shook her head. "I'm afraid it is a wee bit too salty," she said to her sister, Alice, whom she preferred to call Alicia. For Kathy Saint was "precious," and had a sweet, predatory face and what her sister Alice sometimes thought of as a dainty shark's smile. Kathy "loved people." She was lyrical about "people." "More and more and more people!" she would sing to Alice and her husband, lifting her skirts and sailing about any room in which she happened to be. "How can anyone live without PEOPLE?" And her eyes would shine with what she believed was innocent joy in life and her fellowmen.

Her love for "people" did not extend to the cleaning women she employed, who never remained with her for more than one or two days, or the maids she hired, who left within a week, bag and baggage, or the tradesmen with whom she dealt, or the gardeners her husband had coaxed to work for the family. Among these "people" she had a reputation for greed, merciless exploitation, arrogance— what they designated "slave-driving."

She was a pretty woman of thirty-five. No one but Alice knew her age; her husband, Mark Saint, believed her to be nearer his own age, which was thirty-two. She would soon celebrate her thirtieth birthday, as she called it, and Alice was visiting her today to discover, in her forthright manner, what Kathy · wanted for the occasion. Alice did not often come to this house, for a number of reasons, among them a reason so hurting and so full of anguish that she could scarcely endure it, and which no one guessed. For she was in love with Mark Saint, and had loved him from the moment she had met him, ten years ago, when she was only eight, and he was engrossed with Kathy. He had married Kathy a year later; he had just been graduated from his school of engineering, and he was twenty-three, and Kathy was twenty-six, according to her birth certificate, but only twenty-one, according to her own statement. Her parents were alive then, and entered into the deception with her, for they wished her to marry Mark, who was not only in "a profession," but had inherited considerable money from his parents who had died in an automobile accident when he was fifteen. Kathy's parents owned a small but fairly prosperous little hardware store in the City, and they were awed by the handsome Mark Saint; they adored their older daughter, and had left her the bulk of their savings— fifteen thousand dollars—the guardianship of Alice, their house, and their shop. Alice inherited only three thousand dollars. No one thought this unjust, except Alice, and Alice was a child who kept her own counsel and had a wise and cynical inner eye.

Kathy was considered very charming, and even lovely, by those she had deceived into believing her the gentlest, sweetest, most innocent and most loving of women, and these, strangely enough to Alice, were legion. She was of medium height, and gave the impression of slenderness, for her breasts were small, her shoulders narrow and thin, her arms only barely plump, her waist nearly slim. But her belly and her buttocks and her legs were thick and heavy. The first two she restrained with elastic and steel; the latter she hid in buoyant skirts which swished in a very feminine fashion just below the curve of her gross calf. Because of the constant hurly-burly of her skirts—and this was pure art—none of her friends noticed the expanse of her peasant ankles nor the breadth of her large feet. It had been quite a shock to Mark to discover on his wedding night that his bride, after shedding the artful, bouffant gown and petticoats, had the lower body and limbs of a very sturdy and lustful peasant, made for the plow and the field, the churn and the barn. It had taken him several shocked moments to force back his concentration upon Kathy's pale and luminous face, so daintily shaped, so sweet in expression, so lighted by large blue eyes, so exquisite of dimpled chin and small pretty teeth between naturally red and smiling lips, her nose so finely shaped, her hair so purely auburn and curling. Even while concentrating on these charms, the thought occurred to him that he had never seen Kathy in a bathing suit before their marriage. The thought passed. He loved Kathy, who had such a tender, murmurous voice, such apparent innocence, such a rapturous, childish delight in all things, as she herself declared.

In comparison, young Alice was nondescript, as everyone said who understood the meaning of the word. At eighteen, as she was now, she was much taller than Kathy, very much thinner, and possessed of the most graceful body and legs and long throat. But her hair was almost flaxen, and short and dense and straight about her colorless and oddly patrician face, which very few appreciated for its sculptured planes and look of cleanliness and wise purity. Her young mouth, barely touched with lipstick, had a somewhat stern expression, for no one could deceive Alice, though Kathy would sometimes refer to her with a tender laugh as a "teen-ager." How the plebeians who had been her parents had produced such aristocracy no one questioned, for there were only one or two who recognized native aristocracy when they saw it, and Mark was one of them. Where Kathy was "feminine," as her affectionate friends declared, Alice was womanly, and Mark, after these ten years, understood the difference. (Kathy had but one rule in judging women: Was so-and-so "feminine," or was she not? She was convinced that Alice, "the poor, dear child, is unfeminine, I am afraid. Perhaps even a little, just a wee little bit, masculine. Unfortunate!")

Alice's face, her gestures, her exquisite movements, her grace, her honesty, the lift of her head, her sudden, infrequent smile which glorified all her features and removed their delicate sternness, had no touch of masculinity. She was, in all things, in her thoughts, in her faith, in her wisdom, in her inner strength, in her compassion even for Kathy, the most womanly of women. Kathy, in the secret places of her devious and envious heart, in the smallness of her spirit, in her lack of largeness of vision, knew all about her sister, and so subtly belittled her in order to enhance her own stature and blatant "femininity."

Alice envied no one, nor truly hated anyone, except one creature, and he sat outside now, on the kitchen doorstep. She did not reproach herself for hating a four-year-old handsome and smiling child. That would have been hypocrisy, and alien to her nature. She accepted her emotions simply, and understood them fully, without illusion. She did not yearn to have a house like this one, big and expensive, with steep slated roofs, warm brick walls covered with ivy, a spacious garden, several glittering bathrooms, and an extremely modern kitchen. She would have been glad to share a dusty room in an obscure rooming house with Mark Saint, and would have lain down beside him on a rickety bed with joy and contentment, her heart swelling with the deepest of passions and love, her arms held out to him to give him comfort and happiness. But no one knew this, not even the sly and astute Kathy, who preferred to call herself Katherine. She would have borne Mark's children as soon as possible, and not have thriftily waited for four years, "until we can really afford to have one, you know," as Kathy said with her gentle, self-deprecating smile which endeared her to so many of the undiscerning.

Alice's inheritance from her parents, so small and so unjust, had been spent on her education and "care," as Kathy said. But Alice had been educated in public schools, at no expense, and had been graduated, at fifteen, from preparatory school, the highest in her class. She had then gone to Teachers College, and had covered the course in a little less than three years, and now taught school in the City. Immediately upon her graduation she had left this house, to Kathy's relief but vocal reproach, and shared a two-room apartment with another teacher. She did not like the suburbs, she insisted, and this was one of the very few lies she had ever uttered, and it was spoken to remove the hurt expression from Mark's dark and clever face and clear, hazel eyes. But living so close to him was beginning to mean unbearable anguish for her, and even when she visited this house she almost always came during the day and rarely encountered Mark except on special occasions. Moreover, her hatred for young Angelo, as Kathy had fancifully insisted on naming him to Mark's disgust and Alice's unspoken disdain, was becoming too huge for continued silence. (When Kathy first saw her son, two hours after his birth, she had cried, "Angel!" and then had sought a name that would permit her to so call him all the days of her life.)

It was full summer now, and Alice was taking an extension course at the City's university in order to obtain her master's degree. She intended, later, to become a PhD, and then teach in the university, or in another city's college. Marriage to anyone but Mark Saint was unthinkable to her eighteen-year-old and intellectual mind. The steadfastness of her love never diminished, never changed, was never diverted by any other man.

The latest maid in the Saint household was, as Kathy pettishly put it, "lazing away on our time," though the girl was merely exercising her right to an hour's rest after a strenuous day of work under the complaining lash of Kathy's sharp tongue. Elsie's day began at six o'clock, when she had to rise from her bed in a small room on the third floor to bring Angelo's fresh orange juice and vitamins, to examine whether he had committed a nuisance

during the night—which he often did, spitefully, to annoy
the constant stream of maids who came and then left in
bitter anger—and then to give him his bath and coating
of fragrant powder, upon which Kathy insisted. "I want to
keep him a baby as long as possible!" she would carol
sweetly. "A child deserves the precious days of his babyhood, and cuddling, and pampering. They are so short!"
After this coddling, he must then have "his" cereal, eggs,
and mixture of cream and milk. All this was not accomplished without great difficulty, for Angelo had a high
temper and native brutality and the child's instinctive
cruelty and malice which, in Angelo, were accentuated. He
hated the maids; he understood that his mother exploited
them, and degraded them with her condescension and her
general vicious treatment, and so, to him, they were mean
and worthless creatures who deserved tormenting. He liked
to see them pale with anger, or color with frustration
when they served him, or weep despairingly when he was
particularly malicious and detestable. They enhanced his
sense of importance, his belief that he stood in the center
of the world, and that all was made for his own purpose.

"How is Elsie coming along?" asked Alice, standing
near her sister who was anxiously seasoning Angelo's
special chicken broth. The fine kitchen was paneled in
knotty pine, one wall covered with shining copper vessels
of all sizes. Chintz curtains of blue and coral blew gently
at the windows, and the blue kitchen furniture gleamed
with a coating of plastic wax.

Kathy shrugged. She wore a dotted dimity dress the
exact color of her eyes and the furniture, with her usual
fluffy skirts and stiff petticoats which concealed the gross-
ness of her belly and buttocks and thighs and upper
calves. Her lovely auburn hair curled moistly about her
pale and translucent face, and she looked charming, as
usual. The kitchen was hot, in spite of the breeze at the
windows. Kathy glanced at her sister, with a moue of
despair, then remembered that this was Alice, or Alicia,
and that she need not act or pretend. So she frowned, and
said with some surliness, "Oh, she's as bad as all the
others. Does as little as possible. She's sulking upstairs
now, because I insisted that she wash out a batch of
Angel's underwear, and dear little shirts and pants and

stockings. Only about an hour's work in the basement, with our washer and dryer and ironer! But what can you expect of such trash?"

Alice's stern young mouth, which often relaxed into intense softness in spite of herself, became tight. "Don't you have a laundress twice a week, Kathy?"

"Oh, Alicia, how many times must I INSIST that you call me by my right name, Katherine! It's so vulgar to be called Kathy—"

"That's what you were baptized," said Alice bluntly. "Never mind. Go on."

"Yes, I have the laundress!" Kathy clattered a spoon on the sink, with vexation. "But in this weather, really! I don't want Angel's clothing to get the least bit musty, and I do change him so often!"

The boy, outside, hearing his beloved name, lifted his head alertly and tried to follow the conversation.

"But—Katherine—you know that you told Elsie, as you tell all the maids, that they never have to do any laundry. Or heavy cleaning. It isn't fair to demand that they do, after you hire them. And Elsie is such a good cook, and so competent and responsible. And you pay her so little. I often wonder how you get them, honestly!"

But Alice knew. A prospective maid was invariably fascinated by Kathy's air of innocent sweetness, her tender words, her look of melting trust, her promises, her trilling laughter, her affectionate demands that if Mary or Jane or Elsie took the "position," she must, she really must, consider herself "one of the family." Under this spell of sisterly democracy, and the wealth of promises, the hint of not too burdensome work, the selected girl always accepted the position. She remained not more than a month, or perhaps only a week, to leave in indignation and disillusion and sometimes in hatred. If she were foolish enough to give Kathy's name as reference to another employer, Kathy made it her "duty" to enlighten the woman about the maid's incompetence, insolence and sloth, and would even hint of missing lingerie or linen or silver, and all this in such a sighing, suffering voice that the girl was never hired. No one knew of this but Alice, who usually warned the girl quietly not to give her sister's name as a reference.

She herself would write out an appreciative note, and slip a bill into the envelope.

The boy outside scowled, and kicked his stuffed bear, for he did not hear his name. When Alice spoke, he put his hands over his ears, and felt again that spiteful urge to soil himself, and then remembered, again, the one or two occasions when Alice, who watched him between maids when Kathy and Mark were away at dinner, had thrashed him for his incontinence. SHE was talking again, and he writhed a little on the step.

"Do try and keep Elsie," said Alice, while Kathy covered the soup pan with the hushed care of one handling a holy thing. "She's very good."

"Let's change the subject," said Kathy, in her natural voice, which was hard and flat. "You asked me what I wanted for my birthday. You have only your salary, and you're spending your first year's savings at the university, and heavens know why! Well, I'd like an automatic fryer."

"That's about thirty-five dollars," said Alice, in an expressionless tone.

"Yes. Very cheap, isn't it?" Alice thought of the small sum remaining in the bank. This was only the middle of August. She would not receive her first paycheck for over a month. Of course, she thought, I can always charge it, and pay for it in October.

"An automatic fryer, then, it is," she said. Her eyes, a blue much darker than Kathy's, and filled with the radiance of intellect, clouded a little. She detested being reminded of her sister's native avarice. Kathy gave her a peeping glance.

"You really should get married, dear," she said. "You'll soon be nineteen, and it's time for you to be looking around for someone substantial and responsible, like Mark. You'll never realize the joy of marriage until you have a child like Angel!"

"I thought the joy of marriage was in the husband," said Alice dryly.

"Don't quibble. Mark's a darling, of course. But marriage means children."

"Why don't you have another, then?" asked Alice. She was distressed to hear a faint taunting note in her own voice, but she was thinking of Mark, who existed, in

Kathy's mind, as the father of her child and the provider of his comforts and the means of creating a large inheritance for him.

"Oh, how can you say that, Alicia!" cried Kathy, in a despairing voice. "I had such a hard time when Angel was born!"

"And besides," said Alice, and wondered at herself, "thirty-five is a little old to be having more children, isn't it?"

There was a sudden silence in the hot bright kitchen. Kathy's face took on a shade of venom, and her eyes sparkled. Then Elsie, her features set sullenly, entered the room, and Kathy said with sharpness, "It's five minutes after four! You were supposed to be down here five minutes ago!"

"I'm tired, Mrs. Saint," said Elsie. Her tone was ominous, and Alice knew immediately that good Elsie was preparing to leave in a short time. But Kathy never knew, or cared. There were countless Elsies just waiting to be exploited, if only for a few weeks, at a small salary, and most easy to deceive with a beguiling smile and honeyed lies.

"How are you, Elsie?" asked Alice, going to the girl who was beginning to wash some dishes. Elsie looked over her shoulder at the younger girl, and smiled. Now, she thought, Miss Knowles was a really lovely person; you never knew how lovely she was until you'd seen her a few times. Elsie regretted that she would not see Alice again.

"Fine, Miss Knowles," said Elsie.

"Do hurry with those dishes!" said Kathy. "It's almost time for Angel's little snack."

The boy heard his name once more, and he smiled in beatitude. He stood up, reached high for the knob of the screen door and entered the kitchen, stamping his feet loudly. His smile disappeared; he began to whine fretfully, and gave Alice a malevolent look. Alice returned this with a regretful smile. It was dreadful to hate the child. Was it Kathy's fault? Alice silently shook her head. She hoped it was so, and often she prayed that Angelo would improve as children had a habit of improving when the world assaulted them with reality and refused to coddle them as their mothers coddled them, and demanded of them some semblance of humanity and decent behavior, or be rigorously punished.

When Kathy saw her son her face radiated pure light. She swept him up into her arms with a cry of ecstasy, almost lascivious in its undertone. She pressed him to her breast and covered him with kisses. She knew the exact posture to take, legs a little apart, supple waist bent backwards, one shoulder raised a trifle, one arm about the boy just so, the other arm lifted and the hand curled and caressing, to create a charming picture of mother and child. As usual Alice thought to herself, and again with regret, that Kathy was a very amateur "ham." She wondered if Kathy assumed this posture without an audience. It was very possible. Alice regarded Angelo gravely, as his mother kissed and fondled him, and he grinned at her with knowing malice, for he was a very intelligent child with every child's acute awareness of the emotions of adults.

He was much larger than the average child his age, and muscular rather than fat, and he was quite the handsomest boy Alice had ever seen. She taught young children a year or so older than her nephew, and some were handsome and some were pretty. None could compare with Angelo. He had been born handsome, with no redness, no withered skin, no distortions, no simian resemblances. At birth, his hair was as crisply curled and dark red as it was now, his light brown eyes as big and shining, his skin as smooth and fair, his lips as pink, his cheeks as dimpled, his nose as well-shaped, his chin as round and firm, his ears as excellently formed. He had had none of the unfocused stare of the usual baby; almost from birth he seemed acutely knowing. He resembled his parents. He had Kathy's overt charm, her fascinating smile, her coaxing ways, when it pleased him to coax rather than demand with screams of rage. His profile sometimes reminded Alice achingly of his father, and so her hatred was not always steadfast.

"My precious one!" Kathy sang, and began to whirl about the kitchen with the big boy in her arms, her skirts lifting and swaying, her bright auburn hair flying about her face. "My darling! Mother's adorable! Mama's delight! Oo, oo, oo!"

Angelo's gaze never left Alice's averted face, and he chuckled, and when he pinched his mother's check his touch was less savage and deliberately hurting than usual. Kathy kissed the strong, tanned fingers, and threw back her head to let her worshiping eyes look upon her child. "Oh, Alicia!" she sang lyrically, "this is what I mean about marriage!"

She let Angelo slide to the floor, following his passage with kisses on random spots. "Oh, Alicia! Don't you miss him, now you've left him?"

Alice said, "I wish you'd call me by my right name, Kathy." She looked about for her purse, then remembered she had left it in the hall. "I really must go. I have at least four hours' study waiting for me."

Kathy said, in her hard change of tone, to Elsie, who was regarding Angelo with a curious expression, "Take Angel to the powder room. It's been two hours!"

"No!" shouted Angelo, stamping his foot. "I don't want to go!"

"Oh, darling, you must, you must. You know how you love the pretty green potty in the powder room. But would you rather go upstairs?" She half squatted before him, with her head cocked like an adoring dog, her eyes intent and anxious.

"No, no!" he shouted, and beat his strong feet on the coral linoleum tiles. "I want the green potty!"

Can't she keep her hands off him a minute? thought Alice, disgusted. She mauls him all the time.

Kathy squealed with joy at her son's decision, and clapped her hands. She lifted him in her arms again. "I'll take you!" she said in that singing voice, and left the kitchen with Angelo, and entered the large cool hall whose floor was covered with black and white glimmering marble. Alice could hear the quick pattering of her footsteps on the stone, and her constant, murmurous words of endearment. Alone with Elsie, she said in a low voice, "Elsie, this job isn't too bad. Why don't you stay?"

Elsie answered at once, and simply. "You know I'm going, Miss Knowles? Then you must know I just can't stay. I'm sorry, but it's that—that kid. He kicked me twice today, and I've got bruises on my shins. And I can get much more somewhere else, and more time off. Mrs. Saint said I could have practically every evening off, except when they went out, and it isn't so. I have to sit up there with that—kid—and watch him breathe and sing to him until he's asleep, except the times Mrs. Saint wants to sing him to sleep or read to him. Even then, I've got to be around to do anything he wants, if he wakes up. And they have a lot of company, Miss Knowles. Last week, there was only one night when they didn't, and I didn't get through until twelve o'clock, and I have to be up at six. I wouldn't have taken the job, if I'd known," she added, with bitterness. "Too much work; I've got to go every second. If I sit down, Mrs. Saint finds something for me to do. I'm sorry. She's your sister, and I guess I shouldn't be talking this way."

She regarded Alice, troubled. She was a strong, short girl, clean-looking and with an air of self-respect, and her brown hair was neatly combed and her brown eyes were firm and without guile. Alice sighed, and looked at the floor between her feet. Elsie was the best maid Kathy had had to date, a deft and knowing cook, a good worker, and possessed of dignity and pride.

"All right," said Alice. "Of course, you must do what's best for yourself. I understand." She hesitated. "If you want me to, Elsie, I'll write the reference for you."

The two girls regarded each other straightly, and with comprehension. Elsie nodded, and her mouth quivered for a moment. "I haven't told Mrs. Saint yet. I'm going to give her a week's notice tonight. But honest, Miss Knowles, I don't know how I'm going to stand another week! I do like Mr. Saint. He's a real nice man, and considerate, and he always talks to me like I'm a human being, and Mrs. Saint don't. And I thought she was so wonderful when I took the job three weeks ago! That's the kind of a fool I was. I'm sorry, I shouldn't—"

Alice looked about the immaculate kitchen. Every room in the house was immaculate and shining, polished and gleaming. Kathy received her money's worth from her maids and her cleaning women, and she was tireless herself and had a remarkable sense for line and color and decoration. She was the admiration and terror of interior decorators. Everything was of the best quality, unique and distinctive. Like Kathy herself, the house was charming.

Her words might be banal, her intellect not too dazzling, but her taste was flawless. Alice sometimes thought of her sturdy parents, who preferred red velvet draperies and mohair, heavy furniture, and brown thick carpets, and she wondered where Kathy had acquired her flair for the fine, the noble, the appropriate. The girl smoothed her gray linen dress with her hands and pondered. She herself, as she readily admitted, had no such flair as Kathy's.

The older woman returned to the kitchen, laughing, and showing all her small white teeth in delight. "He's growing up, my little baby! He won't let me stay with him any more when he's on the potty! My big, big boy!"

"He certainly is," said Alice wryly. "I'm glad you've remembered that. He'll be in kindergarten in less than a year, or perhaps in first grade, if he ever learns to control himself."

Kathy's face changed. "Alicia. You don't know anything about children, and that's bad for The Children. I have a new book on child psychology; I wish you'd read it. All psychiatrists are unanimous in saying that children get tremendous pleasure from soiling themselves, even when they're older than Angel. And parents shouldn't deprive them of that pleasure too soon. You can ruin a child's life, inflict a trauma on his emotional nature, if you force toilet training on him too soon. Ask any psychiatrist!"

"No," said Alice. "I prefer to ask people who have common sense. Angelo's past four; if he were my child I'd whack him until he stung for hours, and he'd remember after that."

Kathy shrugged, and smiled. "I pity The Children in your class."

"I can tell you one thing," said Alice. "They don't come equipped with diapers. Not even children almost as young as Angelo. No teacher would stand it for a minute, and the other kids would teach him a sound lesson the very first time."

"No wonder so many poor children are suffering mental blocks and have emotional difficulties," said Kathy, with a sentimental sigh. "And have to suppress hostile feelings, and have conflicts. And no wonder we have so many juvenile delinquents."

"Kathy, don't be such a fool, repeating that psychiatric

jargon all the time. You know hardly any more about children than the psychiatrists do. You were Mark's stenographer, remember? And a good one, and you're a fine housekeeper and the world's best cook. Stay within your limits. Now, don't glare at me. I've really got to go."

"Oh, but I want you to see my new bedroom draperies!" cried Kathy, waving away her sister's words as puerile. "Wonderful material. And you couldn't guess what it cost me to have them made up. I'm almost ashamed to tell you."

"I'm sure you got the advantage of Mrs. Sears," said Alice, with no expression on her face. "You always do. She doesn't make a cent, doing your work. What do you do? Hypnotize her, or something? Or do you give her lessons in child psychiatry free? She supports two grandchildren, doesn't she?"

"She gets her biggest benefit from the reputation she has of working for the Saints!" snapped Kathy. "And don't think she doesn't brag about it." But there was no color of embarrassment on her cheeks. "And what harm is there in driving a good bargain and getting your money's worth, or a little more?"

"I'll see the draperies another time," said Alice, turning away. "Besides, isn't it getting late for Angelo's precious little snack? He's been on the pot for some time now."

Kathy rushed to the refrigerator to bring out the daintily decorated cottage cheese mold, the gelatine, pink and shining, and the glass of milk in the gay little jug, for her son. While she was busy laying them out on the kitchen table, Alice smiled at Elsie and went into the large hall, where it was so pleasantly cool, the marble so perfectly polished, the great curving stairway floating up to the second floor. The girl paused a moment to enjoy what she had most willingly left, but still regretted. The walls, of painted ivory, bore a few excellent modern originals in bright and vivid colors, framed exquisitely. At another wall stood a Chippendale mirror mounted over a beautiful console. It was on this console that Alice had laid her purse. It was not there now.

"Do wait a minute," called Kathy, from the kitchen. "I want to tell you something, Alicia."

"All right," said Alice. She was certain she had left her

purse there. Her books still remained on the console; she had put her purse upon them. She glanced at the authentic Chippendale chair near the staircase. But her purse was not to be seen. She frowned. Something caught her eye near the grilled glass door leading outside. The powder room door, to the right, was slightly open. She went to it at once, saying, "Angelo, have you taken my purse?" She knocked on the door, and it swung inward at her touch. The pretty room was empty. Angelo was not there, but on the black-tiled floor lay Alicia's purse.

She looked at it with incredulous shock. It had been opened, and all its contents were scattered on the floor, and all had been methodically ruined. The lipstick had been wrenched from its gilt holder, the holder flattened, the lipstick ground into the tiles. The silver compact, which Mark had given Alice for Christmas, was open, the glass broken, the powder poured out. Its curved lid had been battered by a strong heel and wrecked. The sunglasses had been smashed against the basin, and the plastic twisted and left in a full two inches of water. The little jeweled comb, of which Alice was so proud, floated in the toilet. Her wallet had been opened, the bills thrown about, some in the bowl. One or two had been torn into shreds. Her change purse yawned open; a litter of silver and copper lay on the floor. Her lace handkerchief had been befouled. Her tiny perfume holder lay splintered in fragments in a corner, and the room smelled strongly of the precious and hoarded French scent.

Aghast, and now trembling, Alice sat down on her heels and looked upon the bestial vandalism her nephew had committed against her. What she saw was his rage that she knew all about him: she saw his hatred of her perspicacity, and of herself. This was not simply childish malice, done unthinkingly. It was a horrifying display of something too evil to be thought of, of a malignance too unchildlike. Alice shuddered. She did not hear the hall door open, and she fell forward on her knees as a masculine voice called to her heartily, "Alice! What are you doing there, saying your prayers?"

She was too sick to reply for a moment. There was a huge salt lump in her throat, and a dimness before her eyes. A shiver of desperate coldness ran over her flesh.

Then, still kneeling, she put out her hands to cover, to hide, from Mark Saint, what she did not in mercy wish him to see. She said in a shaking voice, not looking at him:

"Oh, it's too stupid. I—I dropped my purse, and look what happened!"

"What a mess," he said sympathetically, in his kind, strong voice which she loved so deeply. He knelt down beside her. "Let me help you." He tossed his briefcase aside. Then he whistled. He picked up the compact, and examined it. His face changed, darkened, and Alice said quickly, "When it all fell out, I stepped on the poor compact!"

His shoulder was against hers, his dark flannel shoulder, and she wanted to burst into tears. She scrabbled blindly at the ruin of her possessions, and tried to laugh. The sound was almost a moan.

"And I suppose you also tore up those bills," said Mark, in a strange tone, "and threw your comb in the toilet, and ground your lipstick into the tiles, and broke and twisted your glasses and tossed them into the washbowl."

"Please," murmured Alice. "Please, Mark. It doesn't matter, really it doesn't."

"Oh, Mark!" cried Kathy, in a gay voice. "Aren't you home early? What are you both doing there on the floor inside the powder room? Oh, I see. You dropped your purse, Alicia. What a shame."

Mark raised himself on his knees and twisted his body toward his wife, while Alice hastily rescued what she could and thrust it into her purse. She cut her finger on a sliver of glass. Childishly, she thrust the finger into her mouth, and her eyes burned with salt.

"Where's Angelo?" asked Mark quietly. His dark thin face, with its well-cut features and vivid hazel eyes, was set and remote.

"Yes, yes, where's my Angel!" exclaimed Kathy, looking closer into the powder room, and then about the hall. "Oh, that little rascal! He must have gone upstairs." She went to the stairway and put her hand on the banister and sang upwards, "Darling, sweetheart, where are you? Your nice little snack is ready."

Mark got to his feet, and looked at his wife across the black and white marble of the floor. "Kathy," he said. She turned a bemused and radiant face in his direction, and then her expression became pettish.

"What is it, Mark?" she asked impatiently. "Oh, dear. I'll have to go up and find that little teaser. He does play tricks, sometimes."

"Yes," said Mark, still quietly. "He plays tricks. Come here, Kathy. I want you to look at this. This isn't a trick. This is a display of—I don't want to say it, Kathy. I just want you to look at what your son has done to Alice."

"What are you talking about?" demanded Kathy, and her voice was shrill. She tapped across the marble, her skirts swishing all about her like the skirts of a ballet dancer. "What do you mean? What has our baby done?"

"This isn't the work of a baby," said Mark. Gently, he lifted Alice's trembling hands from the floor, and held them tightly in his own. "Look, Kathy. Angelo did this. I can guess why. I don't want to say it, I tell you."

Kathy, with a murmur of annoyance, bent and looked at the wreckage. Her eyes widened. She bit her lip. Then she looked at Alice, and the look was charged with enormous dislike. "What did you say to the poor child, Alicia?" she asked, in a harsh voice. "When you tried to come in here? It must have been awful! Oh, the poor baby."

"Please," said Alice, struggling to keep down a dry sob. "It doesn't matter. Please, Mark." But she let him retain her hands. They were standing close together now, and Alice let her eyes rise only to Mark's tanned chin, and her heart shook.

"What did you say to him?" cried Kathy. "What terrible thing did you say?"

"He wasn't here when I opened the door," said Alice, through quivering lips. "Please don't be upset. It was just a childish prank."

"Why, of course, it was just a childish prank," said Kathy. "After all, he's only a baby. Are you sure you didn't just drop your purse, Alicia?"

"Don't be a fool, Kathy," said Mark. He had never before spoken to her like this. "Look in the toilet; look in the washbowl. I suppose you'll next be asking Alice if she didn't really do this herself."

"Just a prank," insisted Kathy. Her face was quite pink.

"Yes, yes," said her sister. "I think we're all making a fuss—"

Then Mark said in a lashing voice like the crack of a whip. "Get that boy, Kathy! Do you hear me? I want him down here at once. He's out of hand now. I've been warning you about this, and now it's happened. Now that he's acted like a devil, he's going to be punished like a devil, and he's going to get the first thrashing of his life. And from me!"

But Angelo suddenly materialized behind his mother, a beautiful tall boy with an engaging wide smile and big innocent eyes. "Here I am, Daddy," he said, and lifted his truly angelic face up to his father. Mark dropped Alice's hands. Involuntarily he stepped back a pace. "Did you call me, Daddy?" Angelo asked with much of Kathy's sweetness in his childish voice.

Kathy caught him against her skirts, and put her arm about his shoulders. There was something vicious glinting in her eyes as she stared, not at Mark, but at Alice.

"He's just a baby!" she said. "Alicia, you must have said something terrible—"

But Mark put his hands on his knees and bent his legs and faced his son. His features were stern and fixed. He said, "Angelo, why did you do this?"

"I didn't!" screamed Angelo suddenly. "I didn't, I didn't!" And he buried his face against his mother's skirts and beat her arms with clenched fists. "I hate her, I hate her, I hate her!"

"There, you see," said Kathy, in a significant tone. "Oh, dear, now he's perspiring and shaking. He'll be sick all night."

"Son," repeated Mark, but Angelo howled. Alice tucked her purse under her arm, and looked at the door despairingly. But Mark stood between her and flight. She said, "I wish you wouldn't be—like this. It doesn't matter. Children do all sorts of things. I'm a teacher, and I know."

"He's been overstimulated, overexcited!" said Kathy. "Feel his forehead, Mark, and his neck. All wet and hot. Perhaps he has a fever."

"She stim-late me, she 'cite me!" shrieked Angelo, from the protection of his mother's arms.

Mark stretched out his arm and plucked his son from his mother. He swung the boy to face him, while Angelo, still screaming, held out his arms to Kathy for succor. Then Mark seized his shoulders and shook him violently, and Kathy uttered a wild, loud cry as if assaulted, and grasped one of the small and flailing arms. Her face was suddenly white and sweating, her eyes leaping in their sockets, her mouth open. She tugged at Angelo's arm, trying to release him from Mark's grasp.

"Don't you dare, don't you dare!" she panted savagely. "Don't you dare touch him, Mark Saint! Let go of him! He'll have a convulsion! You'll kill him, I tell you, you'll kill him!"

Alice leaned against the wall and shut her eyes and felt sick. Then she heard two hard cracks, almost like shots, one after another, over the screaming of mother and son. And now only Kathy was screaming. Alice opened her eyes.

Kathy was lifting the boy in her arms. Her opened mouth emitted senseless whine after whine and her eyes were dazed and distended. Angelo's cheeks were reddening darkly, but he was silent. He was touching his face, tentatively, and staring without a blink at his father, whose hand was still lifted after the blows.

Then Alice fled, throwing open the door and running down the walk to her little, old car down the street near the curb. She ran as from a most dreadful sight; her heart pounded with speed and pain.

CHAPTER TWO

Alice Knowles came out into a fine spring snow, like drifting sand. It was cool and refreshing against her tired face. She was almost the last teacher to leave the school; a few children were screaming in the adjacent playgrounds, and the sound of their voices was like the scrape of steel against her eardrums. She was so very tired! She had once asked an older teacher, who was thankfully reaching the age of retirement, if children in the first grade had been so wearing and exhausting in her day, and the teacher, very promptly, had replied in the negative. Twenty-five years ago, she had said, when she had taught first grade, it was expected that boys and girls of five and six would behave themselves, conduct themselves respectfully toward their teachers, dress themselves in cold weather and put on their own arctics, and be interested, or at least quiet, at their desks. "Why, they could read very well at the end of the first year!" the teacher had exclaimed. "Now they can't read even in the fifth grade. I don't know. Are we getting more inferior children, in this mass education business, or are parents now more stupid and careless and indifferent than they used to be? I sometimes look at the parents during PTA meetings, and they always have something to say in big, loud voices, and they don't say anything! They want the teachers to be full-time baby-sitters, child psychologists, play-leaders, chorus-trainers, nursemaids and child-adorers. Especially they want the teachers to worship their children, as if there had never been any such magnificent kids in the world before! Education? Discipline? Those are non-essentials. And yet these people have the audacity to blame the schools for their children's delinquency, ignorance and inability to learn! At our salaries, too! Give the kids marble halls and sports, and the heck

27

with subject matter! It isn't our fault; it's the parents'. People get just what they want, and deserve."

But teachers did not deserve the kind of children who were noisily and impudently filling the schoolrooms these days. They did not deserve children of six who were unable to do even the most elementary things for themselves. They did not deserve children who screamed and threatened at the slightest attempt to impose discipline, and who bounded and bounced in their seats, and shrieked and giggled during attempts to teach them. Why did anyone want to be a teacher? Alice thought. It isn't the salary, which is disgracefully small. I like children; I think teaching is the noblest thing in the world, and most teachers think that, too. But the parents have degraded it to the meanest occupation, and the least worthy.

As she did very often, Alice gravely considered leaving the school system. She was well-educated; she had taken a business course in addition to her liberal arts course. She could obtain a position in an office at much more than she was receiving in the schools, various benefits, paid vacations, and in the company of intelligent adults. Why, then, did she stay? Was it a sense of duty toward these masses of young pulpy humans—overgrown, overfed, overindulged, overstuffed with vitamins, slopping with milk—and a sense of duty to the world of the future? If no one attempted to undo the mischief of stupid parents then America, in a decade or two, would be filled with soft and whining men and women ripe for any harsh dictatorship that would guide and rule them, feed and house them, at the expense of their immortal souls and the continuing existence of their free country.

People ignorantly talked of the "few hours and long vacations" of teachers, and their "security." It was true that Alice and the other teachers were ostensibly at liberty after three o'clock. But that was only the beginning of their real work, such as correcting papers, planning lessons, and extra study. If any teacher worked less than ten hours a day then she was a remarkable specimen; she did not exist to Alice's knowledge. The summer holidays were either a period of prostrated attempts to rest, or of working in other employment to make up for the meager salaries, or of studying in institutions in order to become better teachers. Teachers were often criticized for wanness and drabness. "Do they expect us to be glamour girls after tussling with their children for hours?" Alice once asked an older teacher. "And do they expect us to be able to afford French models on our salaries?"

The girl slowly descended the broad white stone stairs of the school, while the spring snow compassionately soothed her tense and weary face. She looked behind her at the school, a fine, rich, two-story building of rosy brick, very modern, very expensive, with tessellated floors, washrooms a Caesar would have envied, gymnasiums fit for kings, a swimming pool of aquamarine tiles, schoolrooms as comfortable and charming as drawing rooms, and a small theater which would have excited envy in actors on Broadway. But Alice's salary, in her first year, was less than four thousand dollars a year, after the deductions for pension, taxes, and sundries. And she and the other teacher paid eighty dollars a month for their tiny third-floor apartment under the roof, sharing a bathroom, very primitive, with two other teachers in another apartment. We're damn fools, thought Alice, with anger. We should demand twice as much money as we're getting; we should demand that parents respect our authority and keep out of our business; we should demand less extravagant school plants; we should demand that no extracurricular activities be asked of us, so that we have the time and energy to devote ourselves to pure teaching, and nothing else. Schools aren't "happiness centers." They are places to teach the young the rigors of reality, the disciplines of living, and above all, as much subject matter as possible.

A few teachers passed her; they were too tired to stop for gossip; they merely exchanged tight white smiles with the girl. Some were old, shabby and bent. Some were beginning to show the intense strain after a few years of teaching; some were as young and confused and rebellious as herself. But all were tired.

Sometimes a visiting psychiatrist would lecture the teachers sternly. They must teach the children "life-adjustment, happiness, social amenities, group cooperation." They must be "alert" for emotional problems among their charges. These were complex days, the psychiatrist would say, letting his quelling eyes rove over the silent women. A child must have a center of security, love and happiness in his school, in the midst of the world's storm and rage and insecurity. What the fool doesn't remember, or know, thought Alice, who knew her history well, is that the world has always been full of storm and rage and insecurity, from its very birth, and that somehow, and with strength and courage and fortitude, the children of the past managed to survive and create civilizations and art and science and maintain and build churches and enforce both the laws of God and men. They learned their first disciplines, their first responsibilities to the world in which they lived, in school. But the parents had demanded a more "modern" approach to teaching, and they had it, and they also had undisciplined, weak, screeching, and exigent children, ripe for crime, for dominance by the unprincipled strong, for atheism. When and where did this adoration for "The Children" begin? Who had told them they were the most important creatures in the world? There was another ominous sign in the schools these days: many of the boys and girls were exhibiting the traits of Alice's own nephew, Angelo Bruce Saint.

Sighing, shifting the books and papers on her arm, Alice walked down the street to a drugstore where she could buy a badly needed cup of coffee. She wished to delay, as long as possible, the return to the chill and dreary apartment in which she lived. The drugstore was already filled with howling boys and girls of all ages, swarming from booth to booth, spilling over the soda counters, snatching comic books from each other, shrilling, laughing, running. Why weren't those great boys and girls in their early teens at home, helping their mothers or earning their own spending money at some neighborhood job? All were overlarge, overweight, overdressed, rosy, empty-eyed, and grinning. This was a lower-middle-class neighborhood; the children looked like the offspring of millionaires, due to the stupid self-sacrifice and vanity of hardworking parents. When they were older, and the great hard world of reality impinged upon them. they would bawl like bewildered and angry calves, demanding of their neighbors and government the same benefits and indulgences they had enjoyed in their schools and homes. To the ruin of America.

Alice was young and strong, and not much older than the bigger boys and girls, and she elbowed a youth and his girl out of the way in the race to the one empty booth. They scowled at her. She sat down and put her books and papers on the table, and looked formidably at the two who hovered indignantly close by. Her stare intimidated them; grumbling and sulky, they moved away, muttering about "teachers." She ordered coffee and two doughnuts, and leaned her weary cheek on her hand as she waited. She closed her gritty eyes and tried not to hear the din in the store.

A man's voice said in surprise and pleasure, "Why, hello, Allie!" She started and looked up, to see Mark Saint, with his briefcase, standing beside her table. He stood there, tall and thin and vibrant, his dark skin flushed with cold, his crisp dark hair sprinkled with snow. Alice's heart rose on a painful yet joyous surge. She had not seen her brother-in-law since last August, eight months ago. She could not speak; she could only smile. He sat down opposite her, and looked at her with affection.

"Just dropped in for a prescription, and there you were," he said. "How are you, Allie?"

"Fine, Mark." The uproar in the drugstore faded from Alice's consciousness. A fine trembling ran over her flesh. The girl came with the coffee and doughnuts, and Mark ordered coffee for himself. Mark said, in a low voice of solicitude, "You look tired, Allie. Anything wrong?"

"No. It's just school," said Alice. An uncomfortable color began to rise in her pale cheeks. "How—how is Kathy? And Angelo?"

"Fine." A closed expression appeared on his face as he bent his head and stirred his coffee. "Why haven't you been around, Allie? We didn't even see you at Thanksgiving or Christmas. Kathy told me your friend, the other teacher, had asked you to spend the holidays with her and her parents in Boston. But you could have come in at other times. After all, we're the only family you have."

He lifted his head suddenly and regarded her with his piercing hazel eyes. Alice hastily glanced away. "I'll come in soon," she murmured. "It's just I've been so busy."

Mark was silent. It was Elsie, on the eve of her leaving

the Saint household, who had come to him to tell him candidly that Kathy had called Alice, after that wild day in August, and had hysterically accused her of many crimes, among them of hating her child, plotting jealously against her child, abusing her child, and attempting to create dissension between husband and wife. Kathy had then forbidden her home to her sister in the future. "I never want to see you again!" she had screamed. "There's always strain and trouble after you've been here, and my nerves are too delicate, and Angel is too sensitive for such things!"

Alice was also thinking, now, of that telephone call. She was not aware that Mark knew of it. Then at Thanksgiving, and then again at Christmas, Kathy had written her gushing and complaining notes, accusing her of neglect, and inviting her as usual for the holidays. Her lack of sensitivity had appalled Alice, who had made polite excuses. But it was Kathy who spoke constantly to Mark of Alice's coldness and lack of affection for her "family." Was she impervious, and incapable of empathy and understanding, or had her call to Alice been merely a hysterical reaction to the events of that August day? Mark often asked himself, as did Alice herself.

"You know Kathy," said Mark quietly, bending toward Alice. "You shouldn't take her seriously. You're her only sister; she loves you, you know, Allie."

"Oh, of course," said Alice, with increasing discomfort. "I'll drop in soon, Mark." But she had no such intention. It would take a long time before her wounds would be healed.

"I insisted on sending Angelo to nursery school last September," said Mark. "And I'm insisting on calling him by his middle name—Bruce."

"Oh, that's wonderful about the nursery school," said Alice. She paused. "But Angelo is a beautiful name. Why Bruce?"

Mark sipped his coffee. "The kids laughed at him in school. They called him 'Angel Saint.' Kids can be very cruel, you know. Angel Saint! I suppose that's what Kathy had in mind when she named him. But listen to how it sounds, for a boy!"

Alice smiled. "Well, it does sound a little fanciful and

precious. I shouldn't have said that. I'm sorry. Yes, 'Bruce' is better. How does Kathy like that?"

"She still calls him Angel, at home." Mark grinned. "I'm hoping she'll get over it, as he grows older."

"And—Bruce? How does he like to be called Bruce?"

Mark did not look at her. "He doesn't. But that doesn't matter. That's his name from here on. A. Bruce Saint."

"Does he like the nursery school?"

Mark was silent so long, and his expression was so remote and brooding that Alice thought he had not heard her. And then he said, flatly, "He isn't at the school any longer."

"Oh." Alice waited. She saw dark trouble on Mark's face, and she wanted to put out her hand and place it over the thin clever hand near hers. Dear Mark! Dearest Mark!

Mark shrugged. "He hated the nursery school. Even after four weeks of it he still screamed madly every morning, at home, and made terrible scenes. With Kathy. And she cried all over him. Anyone would have thought they were being separated forever, with all the emotion and rage and grief, and the tearing at each other. But he settled down quietly enough in the car, when I finally got him in there, and he was all smiles alone with me. It was like shutting off a hydrant, the minute we were alone." Mark shrugged again. "Well. He is only five, you know. But younger kids than he were in the school. And in September he'll have to go to kindergarten. There'll be more scenes, of course. Kathy's already crying about it, and Bruce is already screaming at the prospect."

"Why did you let Kathy take him out of the nursery school?" asked Alice.

Mark said, with no emphasis in his tones, "She didn't. He was expelled. The teachers said he was incorrigible. That's a ten-dollar word for spoiled. The teachers told me he disrupted the school, fought with the children, and—" He stopped, abruptly.

"I'm sorry," said Alice, her heart sinking.

"Oh, it'll be all right, one of these days. After all, Kathy can't hold back the clock; Bruce will grow up. She says the teachers didn't 'understand' Bruce, that he was just more intelligent than the other children. I think she has a point there; the kid is really exceptionally bright."

"Yes," said Alice, with honesty. "He really is, Mark. You remember he walked before he was eleven months old, and was talking before that. Even when he was a young baby he was unusually alert and alive, and full of charm. He could do things at six months that other children can't do at one."

Mark's face cleared a little, but only a little. Alice was thinking of the years she had lived in the Saints' house, and especially of the years after Angelo's birth. She had been only fourteen when the boy had been born. Those four years which followed had been filled with misery, distress, anxiety and pain for Alice. When Angelo, or Bruce, had been only a year old she had detected an eerie look of malicious hatred in his beautiful eyes when he stared at her. She had not believed it, at first; she had been shocked by her lack of charity. But the look returned more and more frequently, and then was never absent when the eyes of the boy and girl met. How was it possible for a baby, and then a very young child, to feel such mature hatred for another, and why? She had always been loving and patient with him, and proud of him, and had bought him gifts, until the last year, when she had come to dislike and then to hate him. A silent and relentless war had been declared between them, to Alice's helplessness. But Angelo, or Bruce, had hated her first. She shivered a little, remembering. Bruce was not really a child; he had never been one. To be mystical about it, he had never been a baby, either. She had encountered his kind a few times in her class, and had referred them to the visiting psychiatrist, who had declared that "the little ones" were emotionally troubled and needed "tender, loving care."

But Alice knew that Angelo had never received anything but tender, loving care from the moment of his birth. Mark almost invariably conceded to any of Kathy's demands; the two rarely quarreled, and then never in the presence of the child. He was surrounded by security, happiness, deference to all his whims, luxury and peace, all the things which child psychologists declared necessary for the emotional health of children. It was the absence of these, the psychologists insisted, which were the causes of emotional disorders in children. Alice recalled that the few children like Angelo, in her classes, also had superior environments at home, with parents who loved them and each other, and who strived to give those children every advantage. The "broken home" hypothesis was absurd. The best children in her classes, the kindest, the most understanding, the most considerate, were the children of widows or widowers, or divorced parents, or separated parents, or poor parents who could give their children only the barest necessities.

There was something sinister and terrible in the innate personalities of children like Angelo which the tender-hearted and well-meaning child psychologists would not admit or recognize. It would upset the dogmas of their lives, the hypotheses on which they lived and drew large salaries from the State. It would force them to acknowl-edge that many people were born evil, and all the efforts of the clergy, parents and teachers could not abolish that evil. Only the Church knew of these, and warned of them. No one listened.

But Alice, looking at Mark now, hoped for the best. It was possible she was exaggerating; she had always been too serious. Angelo would probably grow up to be the first in his class at college, honored and respected, the bearer of scholarships. It was just that Kathy was spoiling him now, poor, foolish Kathy!

"May I give you a lift, Allie?" asked Mark, as the girl began to gather up her books.

"No, thanks. I have my car, parked around the cor-ner."

Mark smiled at her, and his smile was gentle and kind, and her heart lurched with unbearable pain. "I never noticed it before," he said. "You're a very pretty girl, Allie. Any marriage prospects in sight? If there aren't, the boys aren't looking!"

Alice tried to smile gaily. "Oh, no one looks at a teacher!"

"I don't know why. They're just about the finest people in the world, man or woman. I often wonder how they can stand it, or why they teach."

"It's a long story," said Alice, putting on her gloves. If

she stayed a minute more, she thought to herself desperately, she would burst out crying. She was very "nervy"
these days.

"You'll visit us soon, then?" asked Mark, as they
walked out of the store together.

"Of course," said the girl. "Give my love to Kathy. And
to—Bruce."

She left him quickly, and he stood and watched her go
down the street. The snow had stopped; the sky was clear
and hard and blue and the spring sunshine washed wall
and pavement with pure light. Alice walked erectly, her
shoulders squared, her steps long yet graceful, her pale
hair blowing in the nimble wind. She had an air of surety,
of integrity, and even of loveliness, thought Mark, surprised that he had never noticed these things before. He
stood there, watching until she had turned the corner.
Then he felt bereft, and the sun was less bright, the
atmosphere less clear. Something clean and strong and
womanly had gone from his sight, something without
murk or hot exigence and disorder.

Frowning, he went to his car. He looked at his watch.
It was nearly five, time to go home. All at once, a huge
repulsion came over him, without voice or name. He
dreaded going home, dreaded his beautiful house, his
polished rooms, his good dinner, his pretty wife, his handsome son, and even the fire which would be burning on
the hearth.

He remembered, then, that he had felt this emotion for
a considerable time, without admitting or recognizing it,
and it had begun when Alice had left his house "to be
independent," as Kathy had spitefully said. Something
mysterious had gone when Alice had departed. "What the
hell's wrong with me?" he said aloud, as he started his
car.

CHAPTER THREE

The Saints owned a small but pleasant, even luxurious, "cabin" on a forest-covered bluff ten miles from their suburb.

The acreage about the Saint's suburban house was expansive enough, and the secluded and exclusive area was quiet, cool and beautiful enough to be regarded as "country" by the city dwellers. But Kathy, who had been born and brought up in a tiny, five-room house in the city, on a noisy and somewhat dirty poor street, had demanded "country" for her son, and "clean, fresh air, sometimes." So the land, some ten acres from the bluff rearwards, had been bought, at considerable cost, and the cabin built. It was not truly a cabin, but Kathy, in her coy manner, called it so. It was built of thick, authentic logs with the bark still on them, and contained a large living room, full of expensive rustic furniture and ironware, the walls whitewashed and beamed, the big fireplace of fieldstone, the wide-planked floor darkly polished and strewn with handmade hooked rugs. Fake oil lamps stood on maple tables and hung from the walls, wired for electricity. The kitchen was almost as well appointed as the one in the house in the suburbs, with the same knotty-pine walls, and a planked floor gleaming with wax. There were three large bedrooms and two baths, the former rustically furnished with tester beds, hooked rugs and lamps and chests, the latter glittering with tile and chrome. An area of about half an acre was cultivated around the cabin, with flower beds filled with old-fashioned blossoms and carefully tended great maples and oaks bending over smooth grass, but beyond this area were authentic woods, aromatic with pine, carpeted with needles and leaves of many summers, dusky and secret,

cool and shadowy, sweet with trailing arbutus and violets
in the spring, strongly scented with more robust wild-
flowers in the summer, and painted in brilliant colors in
the autumn. It was a year-round "retreat," to quote Kathy;
the Saints frequently visited the cabin in the winter, for
there was a pond a short distance away where Angelo
could skate, and a low hill where he could use his sled, or
the skis he had recently acquired. "A man" maintained
the grounds and the cabin, and lived in a nearby village.
When the Saints came in the summer, for four long weeks
and every weekend and holiday, the current maid came
with them, for rusticity could go just so far with Kathy.
Sometimes she and Angelo would remain behind when
Mark had to return to the City, and spend the dreaming
summer hours together in the heavenly separation from
the watchful husband and father.

Mark would have preferred a place on the seashore, or
where there were running streams full of fish, but Kathy
was adamant. There must be no menace surrounding
Angelo. Mark had pointed out to her that less than three
hundred yards away was the steep and dangerous bluff,
falling sharply away and down some two hundred feet to
a tiny, narrow valley filled with stones and scrub. Of
course, Mark had had the edge of the bluff walled off by
a log fence, the apertures between the logs were not wide
enough for a small body; the fence extended not only just
along the edge but a considerable distance on both sides
where the land leveled; and the drop was easy and could
even be climbed, and filled with trees. But still Mark was
uneasy. He remembered his own love of danger when he
was a boy, and he had visions of Angelo climbing up on
the log fence to look down at the valley and the plum-
colored hills beyond which faded away into a cool mist. A
false step, a stumble, and a small child could tumble down
the bluff, to be killed. The second year he knew he need
have no fear. Angelo was excessively careful of himself;
he was not in the least reckless; he understood the danger
of the bluff fully. He rarely came within twenty feet of it. In
fact, when Mark once wanted to show him the view,
holding him in his arms, he had screamed and struggled
and wrested himself free from his father, and had run,
bellowing, to his mother. Nevertheless, Mark had the fence

periodically inspected and strengthened, for after a rain or a drought the edges of the bluff were soft or crumbly. And he never failed to warn Kathy, who was even more aware of the danger than himself, and who never let her son out of her sight.

Kathy gave what she called "nature studies" to Angelo, who listened avidly, as he listened to all knowledge. But, unknown to Kathy, he did not find the squirrels and the birds and the other creatures of the woods "cute," as she did. He regarded them as weak enemies, to be chased and tormented and frightened. It gave him joy to see a small animal scuttle away at his approach, and the birds rise squawking at the sight of him. Once he had pursued a tiny lost fawn with a stick, until it had found its mother in the woods, and had hidden itself. When, in Angelo's sixth summer, the boy had chased a young skunk with a rake, and the skunk had turned its terrible weapon on him in despair, Mark had laughed secretly and with an obscure satisfaction to himself. After that episode, which had resulted in hours of screamings, fist-flailings, vomitings, sobbings and stampings, and Kathy's anguish and tears, and denunciations of all animals, Angelo always inspected any of his potential victims for the warning white stripes.

At six, he was a big, strong boy, seeming, at first sight, to be at least two years older than his actual age. His handsomeness had increased. He was tireless and quick; he could climb a tree like a squirrel, there to demolish a nest, break eggs or kill the fledglings he found. The birds began to desert the area, and Mark wondered why, in the early dawns, he no longer heard the sweet calls close by, and the flutter of eager wings. For Angelo was careful never to let his parents know of his cruelties.

He had not gone to kindergarten after all, after the first week of tears and rages, and the complaints of the teacher and the refusal of the children to play with him. So Kathy was keeping "her birdling" at home until the age of seven, when he would be compelled by law to go to school. "He needs other kids to play with," Mark had protested. "All we need to do is to pound some civilized behavior and consideration into him." But Kathy cherished what she believed was her son's preference for her company to the exclusion of everyone else's. "He's so mature," she would say. "He can't bear the babyishness of other children, who are so dull and stupid. They bore him to death."

In a way, this was quite true, as Mark admitted. At six, Angelo could read and write fluently, for Kathy had been an assiduous teacher and had delighted in teaching him. He could even draw and paint with astonishing skill and artistry. He was naturally athletic and supple. He looked upon the world without illusion, but also with extraordinary interest. His intellect was sparkling and sure, without the usual superficiality of young children. He was never bored, except when among his peers. His vocabulary was astonishing, and he had a charming, acute and winning way of expressing himself, which captivated Kathy's friends and made them adore him. He passed the hors d'oeuvres at parties with such grace and politeness that adults smiled at him with blissful affection. It was only when he was alone with his parents that he expressed a fierce but cunning hysteria and uncontrollable behavior and almost wild passion. Part of this was calculated to get what he desired; part rose out of the dark places of his personality, primeval, full of self-knowledge and secret, unchildlike thoughts.

When he was pleased with the world and his parents—he was always pleased with himself—no child could be more delightful or more intelligent, or more obliging. Kathy and Mark carefully taught him the difference between right and wrong, with parents' devotion, and he would nod seriously. He understood the difference as clearly as they did. The only departure from their own knowledge was his utter disbelief that anything he desired was wrong, and that those who believed in "good" were sincere. When he finally did learn that they were sincere he was both astonished and contemptuous. He was wise enough to keep this to himself, though he laughed inwardly. He thought people extremely stupid, easy to deceive, absurdly easy to be cajoled.

Alice had permitted herself, a year ago, to be reconciled to Kathy, but she still avoided encountering Mark. Her love for him grew as she became nineteen, and then twenty. A few times, in desperation, she accepted the company and entertainment of other men, but was invariably heartsick afterwards. She lived a solitary life in her apartment, for the girl she had roomed with had married and left the City. Slow to make friends, Alice did not look for someone else to share the apartment. Mark had been invited to become a member of the Chamber of Commerce, and his photograph, showing his kind smile and vivid eyes in excellent detail, had appeared in the newspapers. Alice had cut out the photograph and framed it, and then had placed it in a special drawer out of anyone's sight. But sometimes she slept with it under her pillow, and wept.

Mark was delighted that the sisters had been reconciled, though he saw Alice not more than half a dozen times a year. But he knew that she often visited Kathy. It seemed to him, when he entered his house, that he could detect if Alice had been there; a faint emanation of her personality remained behind, like a clean scent. Angelo did not mention his "dear Auntie Alicia" at any time. The hatred between the girl and the boy had increased in these years; they accepted it. Angelo knew all about Alice, and she would have been surprised to know that she was the only person in the world he respected, for he knew that only she was not deceived by him. But it was a hating, destructive respect, vengeful and waiting. He had no doubt that someday, somehow, in a way not yet emerging from the darkness of his distorted spirit, he would destroy her. No one dared be in his orbit who did not adore, worship, love, cherish and serve him.

Two days before they were all to leave for the customary four weeks at the cabin, Mark said to his wife, "Kathy, Bruce is almost seven. Like all boys, he should have a dog to care for, something his own for which he is responsible. It will be company for him, too." He remembered the beloved Ruff of his own boyhood, who had been his companion, friend, playmate and guardian, and whom he had guarded in reciprocal love.

"Oh, animals are so germy, so dirty!" Kathy had protested. "You know how they soil things, and cover everything with hair, and track mud. What do you mean, 'company,' Mark? He has me—I mean us. He doesn't want anything else."

"Why don't we ask him, and let him make up his own mind, Kathy?"

"I wish you wouldn't call him Bruce," said Kathy petulantly. "It's such a rough name. Angel he's always been to me, and Angel he always will be. All right, we'll ask him. You can be so stubborn, Mark."

To Kathy's surprise and hurt, Angelo promptly declared he would like a dog. Mark would not acknowledge even to himself the immense surge of relief that filled him, or the reason for that relief. But he bought Angelo a loving and trustful young cocker spaniel of a honey color, with great brown eyes limpid as brook water. The boy shouted with pleasure, seized the dog and jumped high in the air, teeth and face gleaming, while Kathy smiled, filled with jealousy. When Angelo had become more calm, Mark talked to him seriously about the little creature.

"You see, son, Petti must rely upon you for everything. You must feed him, brush him, keep him out of danger, keep his water dish filled and clean. He is your charge, just as you are your mother's and father's charge. He will love you, and you must give him love in return, and train him not only to be your obedient dog but your friend. And no boy ever had a better friend than a dog."

Angelo nodded soberly. "I know, Daddy," he said, in his winning voice. "I'll take good care of him."

"I'll help you," said Kathy eagerly. "After all, it's a big responsibility for a little fellow."

"Bruce isn't a little fellow any longer, Kathy," said Mark, with some sternness. "He'll be in second grade before you know it. In fact, he should be there now."

"He knows enough to be in third grade!" exclaimed Kathy, her blue eyes sparkling with anger.

"So he does," said Mark, and ruffled the dark red curls on Angelo's head. Angelo endured caresses from his father with a strange stillness, and a curious glint in the hazel eyes so like Mark's. It was impossible for Mark to know that his son despised him, that he amused Angelo with his sincerity, his simple, kindly ways, and his strictly honorable speech and motives.

"He should take an examination," said Mark. "I wouldn't want him to be with much older boys. I'm not in favor of the 'age-group' business, for people of the same age are often much older, and younger, than their 'group.' But Bruce never had any playmates, or close friends of his age, and older boys wouldn't welcome him too much, if they were considerably older."

Mark reached out to fondle Petti's head; Angelo clutched the dog tightly and the small thing whined in discomfort. Mark brought this to Angelo's attention, and the boy nodded obediently, and ran out of the house with his new charge. Kathy peered through the window and watched the two romp on the lawn, and her face was full of sentimentality. "I hope the dog won't bite Angel," she said, after a moment.

"Petti's only a baby," said Mark. He looked at Kathy's profile, which was illuminated by the summer sunlight, and he thought that she was truly lovely, and suddenly, once, with a kind of sickness, he knew that he no longer loved her. Had he ever loved her? He could remember being charmed by her and her coaxing ways and her sweet smile, and her archness and eagerness to please him and all others. She had not only been a pretty girl, but a "good" one, in the sense that she had been a virgin at marriage. His had been a coarse world of men and war and harsh study; his mother had been a gentle and feeble little creature, very shy and quiet, and so neutral in dress and voice and manner that he had hardly considerd her a woman. He had had no other female relatives. Kathy had seemed to him the quintessence of femaleness, the very soul of femininity, with her soft voice, her coy little gestures, the way she had of tilting her head like a trusting child, her musical giggle, and her floating dresses. When had he, Mark, stopped loving her—if he had ever loved her? When his son had been born, and he had become no longer husband and lover but only the means by which she sheltered, pampered and coddled Angelo in luxury and ease? Or, had he—sickened, and yes he was sickened—of her long before that, when he had detected acid in the sweetness, lies in the smooth voice, and hypocrisy and cheap sentimentality in her words? Sometimes Mark watched the beaming affection on the faces of her friends, wondering if they knew of the spitefulness of the remarks she made about them to him, and even to others. Watching her now, he recalled that never once had

she spoken to him with kindness, compassion or sympathy
for anyone; calamity in the lives of her friends, grief, loss
of position touched her not at all, though she was effusive
in her expressions of sorrow when among the afflicted.
Were the legion of her admirers and devotees as stupid as
he had once been, and were they so easily deceived?

Mark felt the dryness of despair in his mouth and
throat as he watched Kathy preen and peek like a young
girl; she followed the movements of her son and the dog
with her big blue eyes. She made a murmurous sound in
her throat of passionate love. Once she clapped her hands
gaily. Then, smiling, she turned to look at Mark, and the
smile abruptly disappeared, and her hand flew involuntarily to her lips.

"What is it, Mark?" she cried, with real alarm. "You
look so—funny."

She was very acute; what she had seen on her husband's face had frightened her with its starkness, its
cold penetration. She thought she had detected a fierce and
bitter dislike. But that was nonsense! How could she
believe that of Mark, who just worshiped her, who lived
only for her and their son?

"Nothing," replied Mark, turning away, and he made a
gesture as if he were covering nakedness, and was
ashamed. "I'm just tired out; the weather's been too hot
for me."

He left the room and Kathy watched him go, thoughtfully, her eyes narrowed in reflection. She was too egotisti-
cal to doubt Mark's affection for a moment, but there was
an uneasy stirring in her. She sat down where she could
watch Angelo and the dog, and began to think. Mark had
been strange for a long time, she remembered now. Kind,
yes—sometimes tender, yes; patient, considerate, generous
as always. But he had begun to have odd silences. His
lovemaking was infrequent, and had been for—how long
was it? A year, two years, three years? She shook her
head irritably. She got up to inspect her face and hair
in the long mirror in the hall, and to scrutinize her
figure. It was a little dusky here, and masked the faint
lines on her thirty-seven-year-old face, and the light from
the door created a fiery nimbus about her auburn curls.
She had never liked her throat; even in her twenties it had

been somewhat wizened in appearance, and the light here, dim as it was, did not hide the hard wrinkles on it and the coarse texture. She smoothed her hands lovingly over her breasts and waist, which still appeared young; when her palms encountered the heavy buttocks and massive thighs she hastily withdrew them. The harness about them was like armor.

Had Mark guessed that she was older than he, after all these years, and was there some young girl in his office who had suddenly attracted him? No, that was ridiculous. And it was unpleasant even to contemplate. She was his wife; how could he help but adore her as others adored her? Was she not prettier, more intelligent, more interested in community activities and worthy causes, than the other women she knew, and was she not the finest of house-keepers and cooks, and was not this house the best kept of any, and did she not devote herself to her family? What else could a man want?

The uneasiness left her, and she returned to the living-room window where she could watch her beautiful son and the scampering little dog.

Mark was in his room, completing his packing. But his movements were listless, and his despair had him at the throat like a worrying beast. What could he do? Must he live out his life with Kathy? Must there be no real joy and love for him? Must he endure, for endless years, the sticky syrup of that voice? Mark sat down wearily on the edge of his bed, and looked with empty eyes around the pretty "feminine" bedroom, with its light blue walls, its white lattices which were really not lattices at all but decoration only, its deep blue rug, its pale golden draperies, its chaise longue covered with pink silk, its ruffles and its scents. It was all as arch and foolish as Kathy, and as artificial. Mark rubbed his cheek with the knuckles of his right hand. What could he do? He was thirty-four; he might live for several decades, and always with Kathy. Unless, and now he sat up straight on the bed, he remained with her only until Bruce was about ten years older! But did not everyone say that a boy in his adolescence needed his father more than ever before? What would Kathy make of the boy, if she were alone with him? Mark's heart yearned over his son, and the fear he had begun to feel several years ago was sharp in him. He faced that fear now, as he had refused to face it before. There was something wrong with Bruce, and he did not know what it was.

The latest maid, a kind, middle-aged woman, knocked on the door and said, "It's me, Mamie, Mr. Saint. I brought you a drink. I thought you might need it; it's so hot today."

She entered, carrying a silver tray on which there was a tall frosted glass of gin and tonic embellished with slices of lemon. Mark took it from her, gratefully. He said, "Why haven't you taken your Sunday afternoon off, Mamie?"

She regarded him with simple pity; the poor man looked so tired and drawn, and his right eyelid twitched. "Well, we're going away in a couple of days, Mr. Saint, and there's lots to do, and I have to help with the packing, and do my own, too."

She was short and stout and had a motherly face. She was sixty years old, and homeless, and proud, and a widow. Kathy paid her but thirty dollars a week; she did not know that Mark gave Mamie an extra ten in order to keep her. She had been with the family only two months, but even this was longer than any other maid had remained.

"You work pretty hard here, Mamie," said Mark, sipping at the drink. "Don't think I don't appreciate it, and my wife—"

She shrugged her plump shoulders. "Mr. Saint, I've worked hard since I was five years old. It ain't nothing for me to work. I'll be working until the day I die, I suppose. Work never killed anybody. Besides, Mrs. Saint works just as hard as me, around this house." Her face changed a little.

"I hope you'll stay with us, Mamie."

Her deep-colored cheeks suddenly dimpled. "Don't worry. I will. For a couple of more years, anyway, until I can get my Social Security."

They laughed together, and then the telephone extension rang. Mark picked up the blue receiver and said, "Hello?" Mamie left the room and closed the door behind her.

The line hummed, and there was no reply. "Hello?" said Mark impatiently.

Then he heard Alice's voice. "It's Alice, Mark. I was just calling Kathy about something. Is she there?"

Mark heard the front door close, and then Kathy's voice on the brilliant green lawn. "I just bought a dog for Bruce, and Kathy's gone out to watch them play together. I'll call her."

There was a pause. Mark could hear the beating of his aroused heart. "Alice?" he said. "Allie?"

"I'm still here," she said with a little, forced laugh. Then her voice became low and serious. "You say you've bought a dog for Bruce?"

"Yes. I thought it was time to get him one. Make him responsible for something besides himself. Every boy should have a dog. Don't you agree?" His heart felt thick and fast and muffled in his chest, and the hand that gripped the receiver was sweating. What was the matter with him? he thought.

"Yes. Yes, of course." Alice sounded faintly troubled. She hesitated. "Does he like the dog, Mark?"

"Crazy about him. I tell you, Allie, I was surprised myself, for you know the kid's always had the world centered about him alone. Now he'll begin to get a broader view of life, through the dog."

"Yes. Yes, of course," Alice repeated. He could hear her draw a profound breath. "You're leaving the day after tomorrow for the cabin, aren't you?"

"Yes." He could see her face clearly, so clean, so womanly, so gently stern and without guile. He could see the dark blue eyes, so bright with intellect and understanding, and the abundant flaxen hair and the straight shoulders. The vision was so sharp to him that he felt he could reach out and touch the girl.

"Allie," he said suddenly. "Why don't you come with us this year? You haven't been out to the cabin for three years. And you used to like it."

"Oh, I couldn't!" she cried, as if in distress.

"Why not?"

"I—well, I really promised someone—I thought I'd go to Boston for a week or two. Mark, will you tell Kathy I called, if she's busy now?"

"Allie," he said, and did not know how his voice sounded, so urgent and almost desperate. "Come with us,

Allie. Kathy's always complaining that you never accept her invitations. And it's cool out there. Remember how you and I always took long walks in the morning? Allie? Will you come?"

Alice was silent. Something had been said, something had changed, something would never be the same again. The quiet line hummed between them. Mark could not see, but there were tears in Alice's eyes, and she was very white, and trembling. She had heard with her inner ear, and she had heard Mark's desperation, and she was afraid. What was wrong?

"I'll tell you," she said at last, speaking with an effort. "It's only ten, fifteen miles from where I live. I'll come out next weekend, Mark. For a couple of days. Will that be all right?"

"Yes," he said, "it will be all right."

He stood up. He was no longer weary or without hope. He resumed his packing, and sang under his breath, then began to whistle. When he heard his son shout and the little dog bark, and then Kathy's laughter, he smiled. He drank the rest of his drink. He had been heavily depressed, and now the depression was gone. A man without complexities, he did not question why. When Kathy came up to the room he kissed her.

CHAPTER FOUR

"It's really going to be a squeeze," Kathy complained at the cabin. "There are only three bedrooms, one for us, one for Angel, and one for Mamie. When Alicia stopped coming to the cabin, and showed no more interest in it, I sold the studio couch in the living room. Now, what'll we do? We can't have anything delivered away out here on such short notice."

"I'll sleep on the sofa," said Mark. "You and Allie can have our bedroom. After all, it's only for two nights. I thought you'd be glad to have her come."

"Oh, I am," said Kathy crossly. "After all, she's my only sister. But it does make things inconvenient, and Mamie's been sulking since we came. No movies, no TV, no neighboring maids to gossip with, no shop windows to look in, no bingo, no soda fountains, no cronies. And so the extra work might be too much for her, and what will we do then?"

"It's only two nights," repeated Mark, frowning. "And Mamie likes Allie."

"How can you say that? She's only seen her a couple of times. Did you ask Mamie about all that devotion?"

Mark's mouth tightened, and he stared at Kathy. "Allie never makes extra work or trouble for anybody. If I remember right, she used to help you when she came here. And she's young—"

"And I'm old!" flared Kathy.

"Kathy. Don't be silly. Besides, I don't think Mamie is sulking because she misses going into the City twice a week. You've been burdening her too much. It isn't necessary for Bruce to change all his clothing twice a day out here. We're lucky we have someone like Mamie who doesn't object to doing the washing for us between the times I carry the laundry down to the village. But don't put too much on her. Let Bruce get a little dirty every day, and stay that way."

"Germs!" said Kathy. "Don't you know this is the worst season? You have to be extra careful with The Children in the summer; everything must be absolutely sanitary. You know that. All right, I won't fuss any longer. You can sleep on that short sofa if you're so anxious to have Alicia here."

They looked at each other. Mark had colored darkly, and seeing this Kathy was startled. Mark said, "Don't be a fool. She's your sister, not mine. If there's going to be any more talk about this simply call her up and tell her it will be inconvenient. I'm not 'anxious.' But you should be. It's damned hot in the City, and she can't afford much in the way of a holiday."

He went out of the luxurious cabin, and looked about the neat grounds for his son. His head was suddenly pounding, and he blinked in the sunlight. The flowers glowed on the lawns; the hollyhocks near the edges of the clearing were like pink and white flames. The woods beyond loomed in thick, dark greenness. But Angelo and the little dog were nowhere in sight.

Vaguely anxious, Mark called and whistled. There was no answer except the sound of the summer wind in the trees, and the rustle of startled wings. Mark looked up into the trees, and was pleased that there were birds there again. But it was strange how they disappeared shortly after the family arrived. Then Mark trotted to the end of the lawns and to the bluff, with its high split-log fencing. He could not keep himself from fearfully looking down the side of the steep bluff with its fanged rocks and thorny brush far below. Then he laughed aloud. If there was one place the careful Bruce would never go it was to this fence and this dangerous place. Mark stood and lighted a cigarette and looked to the far hills, which were green and gold in the hot light. There was no fishing here, no opportunity to golf, except twelve miles away beyond the village. But it was full of peace and deep forest quiet. Mark sat on the top of the fence and smoked. He felt languid and content as the sun beat down on his bare throat and arms and head. His dark skin was already

"Has Bruce got a dog? I think I saw Bruce awhile ago, on your own land; it's where the trees are thin. And there wasn't any dog with him. He just stood there and looked at us." He colored with discomfort.

His sister, seven years old, was younger than Bobbie, and more forthright. "I guess he wanted to play with us, or something, Mr. Saint," she said. "But we don't play with Bruce. Not after last summer."

"Why not?" asked Mark, with the old dark anxiety.

The children looked at each other, and Bobbie muttered, "Shut up!"

"No, kids, please. I want to know. After all, Bruce is my child. Did he do something wrong?"

"No." said Bobbie loudly. "It isn't what Bruce does, Mr. Saint. It's just Bruce. He came over one day, and we asked him to play in that old barn over there, and he came with us, and he just stood in the doorway and looked at us. It was scary, the way he looked, and Sally began to cry. She was only six then," he added, with superiority.

"Bruce is shy," said Mark, feeling a little sick. "He's hard to get acquainted with. You ought to have helped him."

"He isn't shy, Mr. Saint," said Bobbie resolutely, looking at Mark with honest gray eyes. "He may be lots of things, but he isn't shy. Bruce just stood there in the doorway and looked at us, and we talked to him, and tried to get him to climb into the loft with us, and he never answered. He never said a single word, Mr. Saint. I'm not telling you a fib. He stood there a long time and just watched us, and his eyes were all big, and he didn't say a word. It was real scary. Sally was crying, and I grabbed her arm and I pushed Bruce out of the way, and we ran home."

"But you're two years older than Bruce is, Bobbie. Why should a boy less than seven scare you? You're as tall as he is, and probably as strong. I can't believe that when he just looked at you you were frightened."

Bobbie colored again, but his eyes did not shift from Mark's. "I sure was, Mr. Saint. And it takes a lot to scare me. I'm not even afraid of ghosts."

Mark smiled. Sally said, "He's got the funniest eyes. Real bright and funny, when he stares at you. I hope he doesn't come here anymore."

"He's a very bright boy," said Mark. "He isn't quite seven yet, but he can read and write very well, and draw and paint and do arithmetic as well as anyone in the third grade. And he's lonely. He doesn't know how to act with other children."

"He sure don't," said Bobbie fervently. "Want us to help find your dog, Mr. Saint?"

"No, thanks. He'll turn up. I just hope he hasn't got lost or gone down to the main road where all the traffic is. Give my regards to your father, Bobbie. I'll give him a ring tomorrow."

The children waved goodbye to him, and watched him until he was out of sight among his own trees. Mark could feel their eyes following him. He thought of Bobbie, who would probably be an estate lawyer like his father. Good people, kind people, but dull. Nevertheless, it would be easier on a man to have a son like Bobbie.

But what is it about Bruce that makes me uneasy? Mark asked himself. A father couldn't ask for a more brilliant boy, or a better-looking one. I wonder why I can't forget how he smashed up Alice's purse two years ago. After all, he was not quite five then. He's very obedient, even though Kathy spoils him; I don't have any trouble with him since I slapped him that summer. I can't get close to him; in a way he's mysterious. Oh, hell. I'm imagining things. But sometimes he makes me feel like a bumbling fool, and not any too bright.

He continued to search for the dog for almost an hour longer. But Petti had completely vanished. Mark returned to the cabin, hoping to hear a welcoming bark. But only Kathy and Mamie were there. Kathy explained that "Angel" had been very tired; his skin had felt quite hot; she had taken his temperature. She had examined him carefully, and she was frank about the details. He had no temperature, thank heavens, but she had put him to bed just to be safe. One couldn't be too careful about The Children. He was asleep now. He was worried about the dog. He had cried.

Petti did not return, though Mark sat until long after

midnight on the porch of the cabin and waited, and whistled softly. The next day he went down to the village to put an advertisement for Petti's return in the local newspaper. The offered reward was large. Mark felt a real loss; he hadn't known how fond he had become of the little dog until now. But Angelo was complacent. He smiled at his father and said he was sure that Petti would be found.

CHAPTER FIVE

Alice arrived at the cabin early Friday evening, her little, old car chugging valiantly up the country road. Mark could hear it as it began its ascent; he was sitting, reading, on the wooden porch, and he put down his book and smiled. It was well that Kathy, who came to the door then, did not see that smile. She would have understood it as Mark did not understand it. "Isn't that Alicia's old wreck?" she asked. "Heavens! It sounds worse than ever. Why doesn't she buy a new one; she makes a fairly good salary now."

"Hardly," said Mark. He stood up. "I've been wondering. How about giving Allie one of those little foreign cars for Christmas? They're cheap, they use very little gas, and they're sturdy."

"Oh, don't be silly," said Kathy, as though this was the most preposterous thing in the world. The aroused avarice in her squirmed. "You do get the wildest ideas, Mark. Do you know how much they cost?"

"Yes. I've made some inquiries," said Mark, in the flat tone that usually warned his wife.

But now she was aghast. "In the first place, we haven't any right to waste any part of our son's inheritance—"

"Who earns the money?" asked Mark, and there was a harsh ring in his voice.

"That's quibbling. It's the duty of parents to do everything possible for The Children. The Children are the most precious things we possess. The Children are the future. Who is going to fight the wars, if not The Children?"

"Why should there be any wars?" asked Mark wearily. With anger, he said to himself, But Kathy and I have never known anything else except crisis and war, since we

58

can remember. My parents often said that before 1914 America was a hopeful and happy place, with some reforms needed in working conditions and strengthening of unions, and justice for everyone who worked honestly. And that would have come, without wars and debt and crises and universal hatred, and advancing slavery and regimentation. Why should we Americans permit ourselves to be brainwashed into believing that wars are a necessary way of life, and preparations for wars the only means to a sound economy? That was the road ancient Rome took, to her death.

Part and parcel of this war psychology which had been so cunningly induced in the universal American mind was the blasphemous adoration of The Children. The Spartans, who constantly warred on their neighbors, and induced wars, had been guilty of this blasphemy, too. And in Russia everything was for The Children. The fruit of wars, the workers for wars, and finally, the victims of wars. He, Mark, had seen enough of war to know its cruel and bloody senselessness, its violence against God and man, its violence against all life. "There was never a good war or a bad peace," Benjamin Franklin had said. It should be written on every blackboard in every school in America. Above it should be inscribed: "Honor thy father and thy mother."

The poor kids, worshiped by evil or stupid adults, confronted on every hand by war and preparations for war! They were cherished as were the fatted victims in ancient idolatrous lands, waiting for the smoking altar where their hearts would first be torn out and then their bodies consumed. No wonder so many thousands of them were confused, rebellious, and felt, instinctively, that they had been cheated of their right to peace and tranquillity and joy in the green garden of the world which had been made for them!

Mark shook his head, and stepped down from the porch and went to the top of the road, where he could see Alice's valorous little car floundering in hard mud ruts and raising a cloud of dust. The very sight of it lifted his heavy spirits. He would have a talk with Alice tonight about all the things that troubled him and were troubling him more and more. He walked down the road a few yards, smiling like a boy.

With a last triumphant snort the little car took the final rise and expired with a loud sigh of relief. Alice emerged with her overnight bag. She was dressed in severe white linen, but a scarlet scarf was folded about her neck, and her flaxen hair was tied back with a narrow scarlet ribbon. Mark took the bag and looked at her with delight and a sense of fulfillment. "You look as cool as a strawberry ice-cream soda with vanilla whipped cream," he said. She smiled at him timidly, but avoided his eyes. "How nice and fresh it is here," she said. "I'd forgotten."

Kathy ran down the steps of the porch and embraced her sister with her usual lavish effusiveness, which was not all hypocrisy and pretense. After all, she had been Alice's guardian, and had done her duty toward the girl. "How wonderful!" she exclaimed. "We're so happy to see you, dear!"

Her face glowed with honest affection. Mark watched the two young women, and a gentle feeling came to him for his wife. Kathy's eyes were dancing prettily; she took Alice by her arm and demanded the latest news of mutual friends, and led her into the cabin. "Angel's having his snack in the kitchen," she said. "He'll be out soon, and then we'll have real cold Gibsons and Angel can pass the appetizers. How nice you look, darling."

She herself looked very "nice," in her big skirt of dotted white cotton with a stiff lacy petticoat beneath, and with a blue ribbon in her auburn hair. For an instant she looked as young as Alice. The two went into the large master bedroom, and Mark sat down, lighted a cigarette, and contentedly resumed his reading. But mechanically, he would lift his eyes and look with hope for the return of little Petti. There had been no answer to his advertisements. Angelo materialized suddenly at his elbow, and Mark started. "I wish you wouldn't creep around like that, without a sound," he said, annoyed.

Angelo laughed indulgently. "I have crepe rubber soles, Daddy," he said, and displayed them. "Should I shout or something?"

"I suppose I'm unreasonable, but you have a way of popping up out of nowhere," said Mark, and patted the boy's strong bare arm which was already browning. Angelo sat on the railing of the porch and contemplated his father with curiously glinting eyes. He said, "I wish SHE hadn't come."

"You mean your Aunt Allie? Why not? Don't you like her?" Mark frowned.

Angelo yawned, but his eyes never left his father, and Mark, to his surprise and vexation, found himself flushing.

"She doesn't like me, and so I don't like her."

"Nonsense. When you were born she was like a little girl with a new doll. She made your christening dress by hand. She didn't have a large allowance, but she spent it for years on you. She wheeled your buggy through all the streets, proud of you. She stayed with you nights when she should have been out having fun like all the other girls. She dressed and washed you, and taught you to walk. She loves you."

"She doesn't like me," said Angelo, with calmness. "And so, I don't like her. She isn't very bright, either. She's silly."

"What makes you think Allie is silly?" asked Mark, forcing himself to smile paternally.

Angelo swung on the railing and meditatively continued to stare at his father.

"She expects things of people," he said.

"Such as what?" Mark was disturbed.

Angelo yawned again. He said, "Too many. That's what makes her stupid." He jumped down from the railing, and Mark's dark eyebrows drew together. But Angelo was smiling at him with all his dazzling charm, and even Mark was not immune to it.

"You forget you're still a child," he said hopefully. "You haven't had much experience. When you grow older you'll understand that Allie is one of the most honest people in the world, the most intelligent, the most just and kind."

Angelo continued to smile, but now there was an odd gleam in his eyes. But he said in his spuriously sober tone, "Yes, Daddy." He looked over the lawns. "I guess Petti won't ever be back. He must have gone down to the main road and been picked up by someone."

"I'm afraid that's what happened," said Mark. "Would you like another dog, Bruce?"

"I think I'd like a cat this time," said Angelo. "Mum would, too. They're cleaner than dogs."

Mark rocked in his chair. "I wish you'd make friends with Sally and Bobbie," he said. Angelo swung to him abruptly, and his motions were feline. He said, "I tried. But they made me go away. I really tried, Daddy. I went over there last summer, and they acted very funny, when I was just watching them play."

Mark did not know why he felt fresh relief. Of course, Bruce was too intelligent to play easily with other children. He said, "Play may seem foolish to you, son, but try to learn to do it. You'll have lots of time to be a man."

Alice came out of the cabin. She had changed her clothing. She wore a simple white shirt with short sleeves, open to show her smooth white throat, and gray linen Bermuda shorts which revealed her long, slender legs, beautifully formed and graceful. She smiled uncertainly at Angelo and said, "Hello, darling."

"Hello, Aunt Alicia," he said with precise courtesy, and suffered her timid kiss on his cheek. "I hope you'll come often."

He ran down the porch steps then and disappeared around the corner of the cabin. Alice took his place on the railing, and twisted her slender body to look over the gardens.

"Kathy was telling me how the little dog got lost," she said, in her low voice. "I'm sorry. Does Bruce miss him?"

"Yes. He was very upset for a couple of days. But he's only a child. He's forgetting now."

A silence stepped between them and held them motionless. Mark gazed at Alice's cool and beautifully cut profile. Her lips drooped as if with sadness; her eyes were tired. One hand rested on her sleek thigh; it had a gentle but abandoned look, a lonely curve.

Then, like a blaze of bitter and blasting light, the thought came to Mark: I love Alice. I've always loved her. And I never knew until now. God help me.

As if the terrible thought had reached Alice she turned her head sharply to him and looked straight into his eyes. The blueness in hers widened and deepened.

Then Angelo was there again, arriving soundlessly, and he was looking at them and faintly smiling, and they did not see him. He watched them for long moments.

"Is there something wrong Allie?" Mark stammered, appalled at his thoughts, and wanting to stifle them.

"No. Nothing, Mark," she answered, and she stammered also. "But I'm thinking of leaving the school system after all. I love it, but I can't stand it any longer. We can't discipline the children; we can't punish them. We can't even give them their rightful rating on report cards. We mustn't hurt their tender psyches, you know, or encourage competition." She paused. "There's some talk in school about sifting out the bright children and putting them into harder classes, with more subject matter, and advancing them as fast as they can go, and giving them challenging assignments. But it's still only talk; the parents in the PTA are vociferously against it. That is, the parents with only average or sub-average children. They say such a plan is not 'democratic,' not fair to the others. But I think it certainly isn't 'democratic' to hold back the best to the level of the inferior."

Her face flushed with quiet passion. "I'll stay, if I'm given a superior class. I have my master's now. I can teach older children. I've already talked with the principal, Mr. Chapman, and he agrees with me, but he's helpless. So, I'll resign as soon as school opens unless I get what I want, PTA or no PTA. The other teachers agree with me, too, but they're cowed by the parents. You know what I'd do if I could, Mark? I'd do what they do in some private schools—just have a sort of general meeting once or twice a year between parents and teachers, to check on the children's advancement, but no interference on the part of the parents."

"You could teach in a private school," said Mark, nodding sympathetically. He had control of himself now. But it was like holding a tiger back in its cage.

"I'm looking for one. I've been offered an opportunity in Boston."

"We won't see you often, then."

She smiled gently. "Oh, Boston is only a four-hour drive from the City." She turned her hands on her thigh and contemplated them. "There's just one thing that keeps me from definitely making up my mind. There's a little boy, about Bruce's age, in my class. He's older than the others; he didn't come to school as early as he should have. It wasn't his fault. It's a terrible thing for Kennie. His father was a drunken laborer; two years ago he murdered Kennie's mother, and Kennie was the only witness. He almost went out of his mind. His old grandmother took him, out in the country, and that's why he didn't come to school. And then he was under treatment, too, in a hospital. He's a very sensitive boy. He has nightmares. He's in a good foster home, but it's poor, and the City pays very little for his support. The thing, Mark, is that Kennie is not only a brave and understanding child, but he is exceptionally bright. He caught up with the other children in only two months. I'm teaching a second-grade class now, as well as a first-grade class, and he's in there, and I think he should be in fourth grade. But that would be 'advancing' him out of his age-group, and encouraging him to 'compete.' I'm going to fight for Kennie, Mark."

Mark smoked, frowning. "My father used to say, 'What's bred in the bone is born in the flesh,'" he said. "The boy's father was a drunken murderer. He's probably inherited a lot of his traits. Be careful, Allie."

"I agree with your father, Mark," said Alice. "But you must remember we all have thousands of ancestors. And traits have a way of skipping generations, and even being bred out. Criminals suddenly rise out of the 'best families.' You've only to read the newspapers. Sometimes the most healthy and moral people give birth to psychopaths."

To Mark's surprise, she turned very pale, and looked away. She said hastily, "Well, anyway, I'm going to do everything I can for Kennie. I'm buying him some good clothes for the fall term; I visit him often at his foster home.They're middle-aged, childless people, and they love Kennie. His nightmares are getting fewer all the time. I buy him books; he's beginning to read Dickens wonderfully. I take him on picnics and to the zoo, and the museums. You'd be surprised how intelligent he is, and how he understands. Oh, if it weren't for Kennie I would have resigned in February!"

She rubbed her hand on the railing. "I've already talked with the social worker who is in charge of Kennie's case.

I've suggested that if I go to that private school I'd be glad to pay for Kennie there. Do you know what the silly woman said? She actually declared it would be removing Kennie from his 'normal environment,' and that it would emotionally disturb him! Are these people trying to create elite classes in this country, Mark, and are they beginning to teach children that they should remain in their 'station,' as they do in Europe? I'm afraid they are! Don't laugh."

"I'm not laughing," said Mark grimly. "I've suspected that for some time. That's why I want Bruce to go to a public school, but Kathy won't permit it. Bruce must be with his 'group,' she says, among children with his own advantages." He puffed at his cigarette; neither of them saw Angelo, in the shadow of a tree, listening acutely. "There's something very wrong going on in this country, Allie. The old and ancient tyrannies and turns of mind of Europe are showing up here, at last. Some people call it Communism, but it's centuries older than that."

"Well, I'm going to fight for Kennie, and for all the other Kennies," said Alice, with resolution. "They're not going to be smothered down in mediocrity and kept in a 'lower class,' if I can help it, no matter how poor their parents are."

"I know somebody of influence in the School Department in the City," said Mark. "I'll write to him, tonight."

"Oh, Mark, will you?" cried Alice joyfully.

Kathy came swirling out with a tray of cocktails. "Where's Angel?" she said. "Oh, there you are, darling. Do go into the kitchen and bring out the appetizers, like a good boy." When Angelo had obediently entered the house, Kathy said lovingly, "It's remarkable what social poise the baby has. He's like a little man."

Angelo appeared with the tray of cheese and crackers. He presented it to Alice with a deep and ostentatious bow; his beautiful eyes shimmered with mockery and secret and hating amusement. "Look at him!" caroled Kathy. "He's like an eighteenth-century gentleman, isn't he?"

Alice and Angelo looked into each other's eyes in absolute stillness for a moment, and then the boy presented the tray to his mother.

He's a horror, thought Alice, and despised herself, as

usual. But I can't help it! He's unclean. When I think of little Kennie, and then look at Bruce, it makes me sick. St. Michael and the serpent. What am I thinking? But I looked in his eyes just now. . . . She shivered.

"When you come again for a weekend, bring Kennie," said Mark suddenly.

"Who's Kennie?" asked Kathy, with her strained brightness. She smiled at Alice coyly. "A prospect?"

"No," said Alice. She briefed her on Kennie's history, and Kathy's face was appalled. Alice hoped, and not for the first time, that her sister was touched, and that she, who declared that she loved all children passionately, would be grieved for the boy and would second Mark's invitation.

"Oh, but we couldn't have a child like that here!" cried Kathy. "His parents! Think what an awful influence he would be on Angel! I shudder to think of it! A murderer's child! Associating with Angel, who's so innocent and still such a baby! I'm so careful of everyone Angel meets or plays with! Honestly, Alicia, what an idea!"

I should have known, thought Alice bitterly. Women who sing about The Children mean only their own children. They detest those of other women. I was a fool. I've known Kathy long enough, God knows.

"We won't even discuss it!" exclaimed Kathy. "It's too awful."

"Yes," said Mark, in a hard, loud voice. "It's too awful."

His eyes met those of Alice's, and he felt a shock go through him again, and he knew that from this time forth he would never know peace or happiness.

CHAPTER SIX

On Sunday morning Kathy and Mark went down to church in the village, and Mamie went with them. Kathy did not believe that Angelo was old enough for Sunday school as yet. "And then, the village children!" she said. "They're awfully rude and dull and coarse, you know."

"I thought God was in every church," said Alice, "no matter what incomes the people have, or whether they're city people or country ones."

"You're always begging questions," said Kathy pettishly. "You really know what I mean. Anyway, I'm grateful you're staying with Angel. Mamie was getting sullen because she was missing church, and now she's pleased."

They drove off, after Kathy had given Angelo a flurry of maternal kisses. She promised him some special candies from the drugstore in the village. "Take care of Aunt Alicia, darling!" she sang, waving to him from the car. He waved back. He stood on the porch in his white linen shirt and fresh long trousers, his dark-red hair shining in the sun, his beautiful face truly angelic.

"What shall we do, Bruce?" asked Alicia awkwardly. "Do you want to play checkers? Or shall I read to you, or do you want to play ball?"

He turned to her and gave her a glowing smile. "Oh, nothing, Aunt Alicia. You're supposed to rest, aren't you? I can amuse myself."

"Well, how about a walk in the woods?" she asked.

He shook his head regretfully. "I just don't like them anymore, since Petti was lost there." His lip quivered. Alice looked at him keenly. Was this pretense, or the truth? She hoped it was the truth.

"He must have been a nice little dog," she said tentatively.

"Oh, he was! He was my playmate and companion. We had lots of fun together. I just can't stand the woods now. I keep looking for him, and it's no use. Someone stole him."

He sat down on another chair and picked up a book. He was soon absorbed in it. Alice studied him covertly. She prayed in her heart, Please, dear God, let me be wrong about this child, for dear Mark's sake. Please let him be better than I feel he is. Please help me to stop hating him.

She got up. "The woods look so cool and pleasant," she said. "Do you mind if I take a walk in them myself, Angelo? Do you mind being alone for just a little while?"

"Oh, I don't mind at all, Aunt Allie," he said, smiling at her tenderly. "Don't worry about me."

"You won't go near the bluff, Bruce?"

"Oh, no. Daddy and Mum warned me about it. And I always mind them, you know."

He spoke like a boy many years older than himself, and his manner was adult and contained. Alice still hesitated. She looked about at the peaceful gardens blowing in the sun and cool wind. There was nothing here to threaten a little child.

"I'll only be about ten minutes," she said, and went down the porch steps, then across the lawns, and into the woods.

When she arrived in the dark shelter of the trees she was astonished that she should feel that she had escaped from something menacing. She laughed at herself. She wandered over the aromatic needles and rustling dead leaves; she sat down for a few moments on a large and mossy stone. The trees met over her head like a dark-green benediction. And then she could not help it. She began to think of Mark, and very slowly, tears ran down her cheeks, and she sobbed a little. She should never have come here this time. When she left tonight, she would make it a point never to see Mark again. In spite of Kennie, she would accept the invitation to the school in Boston. She could always keep in touch with Kennie's foster parents, and they could bring him to Boston to visit her, at her expense, and she could call him and write to him. Dear little Kennie, with his deep gray eyes, his gentle manners, his wise trust, his silences, his eagerness to please, his quiet voice! Even the most malicious children loved Kennie; he was a favorite with everyone. Alice forced her mind to remain on Kennie, but her heart was one great wound of pain and suffering.

She stood up and wandered off again, the resinous breath of the woods soothing against her hot cheeks. It was so silent here, so peaceful, with the sun glinting occasionally through the trees. She listened to the soft and timid rustling in the branches, the little scufflings of wild creatures. She whistled to the birds, and some answered. A squirrel ran down a tree trunk and looked at her inquisitively. She wished she had brought some peanuts. The squirrel regarded her with bright wild eyes, and did not move as she passed within touching distance.

There were vague narrow paths through the woods, made by the family and animals. She walked along them. Then she turned and plunged deeper into the woods. Suddenly she heard the snapping of a twig, or the roll of a stone. City-born and bred, she swung about alertly, dimly frightened. But there was nothing around her but the trees. She was imagining things, or a larger animal had run through the brush. She continued on, and very slowly a peace came to her. She sat down on her heels to examine a clump of jack-in-the-pulpits. Again, she heard that snapping, furtive and sudden. She stood up and called, "Bruce, is that you?" But only the birds answered, and the squirrels scolded. Was it her imagination, again, that made it appear to her that there was a note of fright in these wild voices, or anger? Were there bobcats here, savage and watchful, ready to pounce down on her from some tree? She looked up into the branches; they moved very slightly in the wind. No threatening eyes stared down into her own.

I'm certainly a city girl! she thought. These are only natural sounds. Didn't Mark once tell me there were deer here, sometimes? Of course. It was probably a doe, or her fawn. But still, there might be prowlers, and she thought suddenly of Angelo, alone on the cabin porch. Tramps! She listened, achingly. The woods were utterly silent. She turned about, to return to the cabin. And she bent and caught up a fallen little branch. Her heart began to beat fast.

It was then that she became aware of a sickening stench close at hand. Skunks? No, she had smelled that effluvium years ago, when she used to visit her sister. This was an odd and vile smell, sweetish, rotting. She could not recognize it. Did other animals have warning stenches, besides skunks? All at once, she was unaccountably frightened. She stood absolutely still, like any of the wild creatures about her. The stench deepened; it was almost at her feet. She did not know why she scraped aside a damp carpet of needles and leaves, with one fastidious foot. But when she had scraped the carpet aside she saw that the black earth had been disturbed, and it was a little mounded. Then she jumped in horror. A tiny stiff paw, the color of honey, stuck up just a little from the earth, as rigid as wood.

She uttered a faint cry. She bent and touched the furred paw, and saw the infant nails of a small dog. Then she was kneeling, and frantically pulling away the loose earth with her hands, digging her fingers deep into the soil. The little grave was shallow; within moments the decaying body of little Petti lay before her, and she saw the glazed eyes. And she also saw that the fur was stiff and matted with blood and that the head had been crushed.

"Oh, my God!" she cried, aloud. She fell back on her buttocks and sat there, shuddering violently. She did not hear a distant snapping, and the sound of rapid stealthy feet, retreating.

A long time passed, and she crouched there, as motionless as the small corpse of the dog who had been so cruelly murdered. She knew. She knew at once, with a dreadful clarity. Her mind did not scurry around, desperately, seeking other explanations. She knew. She remembered that Kathy had said that perhaps it was just as well that Petti had disappeared; he had "bitten" poor little Angel. Yes, she knew. She was almost as cold, now, as the innocent corpse rotting there in its grave.

Then, with shaking hands full of tenderness and pity, she covered the dog again with the compassionate earth, and brushed leaves over the grave. Mark must never know. Above anyone else, Mark must never know! And she must say nothing. She must never speak of this, not even to Angelo-Bruce. She took painful care, now, that the earth was mounded over the stiff paw, and that the carpet of leaves and needles was deeper.

She wiped away her tears, childishly, on her forearms. She picked up some wet leaves and rubbed away as much soil as possible from her hands. Then she stood up. She felt desperately ill. And then anger seized her, and a most terrible rage and hatred. And an abysmal fear.

She ran from the woods. When she reached the edge of them she saw Angelo sitting quietly on the porch, still reading, his head bent studiously. It was he, then, who had followed her. She knew this immediately. It was no innocent animal who had snapped twigs or rolled stones. It was Angelo. The rage seized her again and shook her. She felt she was smothering.

She walked very slowly to the porch, over the hot grass, past the blowing flower beds. She reached the steps of the porch. Angelo looked up brightly, and showed all his white teeth in a pleasant smile.

"Did you have a nice walk, Aunt Alicia?" he asked in that loathsome, winning tone.

Alice stood on the lower step and gazed at him, and her dark blue eyes were full of fire and knowledge. Angelo regarded her coolly. Girl and boy stood and sat without moving, and understanding leaped between them like an electric charge. Angelo smiled again. And then, suddenly, he threw back his head and laughed gaily. And then, as abruptly, he was no longer laughing or smiling.

"Mum," he said, in a distressed and beguiling voice, "says you're too old for shorts, Aunt Allie. She says they're just for young girls. Oh, I'm sorry. I shouldn't have told you. They're awfully pretty, and I like them."

Alice stood there and looked at him, and the blue fire of her eyes filled her face with a kind of blaze.

I must go away, she thought, or I'll take hold of him and beat him almost to death. I'll slam his face and head against the wall! I'll twist his throat. I'll pound him into the earth, as he did Petti. Her hands clenched at her sides. Her body became rigid. And Angelo watched her, his hazel eyes welling and alert, his hands palm down on his book.

"Why don't you go away, and never come back?" whispered Angelo, and the whisper was sibilant in the intense quiet. "What are you doing here? Mum and I don't want you. Daddy does, but that doesn't matter, does it? Daddy's very stupid."

The full impact of what he had said did not reach Alice for several dreadful moments. She looked into eyes fathomless with evil age, with ancient understanding of terror, with mockery. And she retreated backwards, several steps, and put her hands to her cheeks.

Then she fled. She ran to the bluff, and arrived there, panting, covered with sweat. That was not a child there. That was a monster! And more and more of these monsters were being born! Had evil finally broken through from hell and was it now afflicting the earth? She put her hands on the log fence and shook her head dazedly. What would the Kennies of this world do with them, the Kennies who were all kindness and compassion and decency, convinced of the innate goodness of mankind, convinced of the ever-loving presence of God? There was only one thing to do with them, and the Kennies were incapable of it, in their pity and gentleness. Yet, at last, and finally, good and evil must inexorably face each other and fight it out to the death. The final hour had arrived in the world, this most portentous world, when the battle must take place.

Weak and undone, Alice sat sideways on the fence, her breath hard and fast, the sweat rolling down her cheeks, mingled with her tears. She twisted her body sideways and looked at the distant hills. And, she thought, Mark must be spared this knowledge. Mark must never know. This would kill Mark.

Alice was silently but intensely religious. She looked at the sky and prayed for the Kennies and the Marks, the multitudes of the good who would not understand, even when the battle was joined, the true nature of their foe. If they defeated that foe they would in mercy try to explain away the evil they had encountered and conquered. They would chatter of environment; they would speak of "no opportunities to be better"; they would talk of "bad leaders who betrayed their people." To the Kennies and the Marks it was impossible to admit that there was true evil in the world, and that it often came clothed in brightness. For the first time in her life Alice, often skeptical and very rational, entertained the idea of a personal Satan just as there was a personal God. There could be no other explanation of those who came like the serpent, fascinating, full of charm, persuasive, eloquent, frequently superior to others in physical appearance and mental endowments. They were counterfeits of the good, and that man was wise indeed who could tell the difference. But the Church knew! She talked of those who were possessed, of demons.

She heard the faintest sound behind her, but she was too late. Even in the very motion of turning her head she felt the violent push against her shoulders. It seemed to happen slowly, as if in a dream. She was tilting dreamily forward; she was looking straight down on the toothed rocks and the murderous brush far below; she was sailing slightly in the air. Then her instinct of survival rushed to her aid. Somehow, as she dropped, she caught a strong stake which supported part of the fence, and she was hanging over the gulf by her right arm, her hand clutched about the stake. Her whole body shuddered abruptly, stopped in the instant of falling; the bones screamed in their sockets; her shoulder exploded into fire; her legs and torso dangled in space, and she was looking at the brown and crumbling face of the bluff, and its dust was in her nostrils.

CHAPTER SEVEN

A wind rushed up from the bottom of the bluff, and Alice's body swung idly. It had happened an instant ago; it had happened hours ago. Only the agony in her arm was real. The muscles slipped; ligaments ripped; her wrist was strained unbearably. She felt her hair fluttering about her face. Then terror took her and shook her as with giant teeth. Only the frail bones and flesh of her right arm held her from death.

Then she screamed. She looked up, her eyes starting. Angelo was leaning on the fence and smiling down at her. Only his head was visible, his beautiful, wicked head.

"Why don't you let go, Aunt Alicia?" he asked softly. "You can't hang there very long, can you? They won't be home for nearly an hour yet. Can you stand it?"

Alice screamed again, and her voice was carried away in echoes, and the sun struck the top of her head and her body swayed and she coughed, as she inhaled dust. She had no thought except to live. She did not even feel horror, for she had accepted it.

"Poor Aunt Alicia," said Angelo, sighing. "She was sitting on the fence, and then she lost her balance and she fell, and I came running and screaming, and there wasn't anyone to help, and I'm too young and little to help her. And there is Aunt Alicia at the bottom, all torn up by the rocks and the brush, as dead as Petti."

Alice made no sound. She looked up into that angelic face with its gleaming smile. Then the smile was gone. A vicious darkness clouded the hazel eyes.

"Why did you have to find him?" he whispered. "Why did you go poking around? Did you know I'd killed him because he was stupid, and he bit me? He bit me on the arm. You knew I'd killed him, didn't you? Well, you're

74

not going to tell anyone; you're not even going to know it yourself pretty soon."

Alice coughed again. Her arm was becoming numb, but the pain was vivid beyond endurance in her shoulder, in her straining back muscles, in her neck. She was sheeted in flame. Then she said, almost as quietly as Angelo had spoken:

"Yes, I knew all the time you'd killed that little dog. I knew it, somehow, even before I found him. I know all about you—Angelo."

He nodded. "And I know that, too. And that's why you're going to drop down there soon. And you won't be around to tell anyone."

I can't die! thought Alice wildly. Somehow, somebody might suspect; Mark might suspect! The police might start to think. They have ways of finding out things. For Mark's sake I mustn't die, please God, I mustn't die! If I do, then he'll know!

"You thought you'd take Daddy away from Mum, didn't you?" asked Angelo. "You thought you'd put Mum and me out of the house, and live there, our nice house I like so much, and all the nice things in it. You thought you'd get Daddy's money. And Mum and I would live somewhere else. I've been watching you and Daddy. You look at each other. Mum's silly, and she doesn't know, but I do! And that's another reason you've got to fall down there, and die."

Alice's eyes were blue circles of light as she looked up at the monstrous child. There was no use in arguing with him; he had no concept of right and wrong to which to appeal.

The girl's body swung gently. "Do you want me to get a stone and hammer your hand away?" asked Angelo reasonably.

"If you do, they'll find the marks. The police are very good," said Alice. She was growing weak. But she had a thought. She must keep him occupied so he would not see. Stealthily, her left hand crept to her wide leather belt. It was too large for her; she had intended to cut off the extra inches this morning, but had forgotten. She thanked God for that forgetfulness now. Tears slid along her eyelids.

"Yes," she said, "the police always suspect everybody in an—accident. They search; they look; they always find clues."

"But I'm just a dear little boy," said Angelo, grinning down at her. "I'll be hysterical; I'll get a fever; Mum will have to put me to bed and call the doctor. The police won't even think of me, I'll be so sick."

He reached down and then rose again and showed her a jagged stone. "It's sharp," he said, looking at it with critical approval. "And I can kneel down and push my hand, with the stone in it, through one of the slits in the logs."

"And the police will find fragments of it in my flesh," said Alice. "Don't think for a minute that the police won't search. And they're on to children like you, these days. They think of them first now; they'll especially think of you, when they know we were alone. And they'll go through the woods, and they'll find Petti. The police never let up. And they'll talk to people who know you, the schools you went to, the neighbors' children who won't play with you. And then you'll be taken away and you'll never see your mother again." She dared not glance down into the giddy nothingness below her.

Torturous movement by movement, she had undone the belt. Now it was free in her trembling hand. It was heavy leather, not plastic; it would hold. Angelo's face had changed during the time she had been speaking. It had darkened; he held the rock tentatively.

"They'll put you away with your kind," said Alice. "They know all about you! You'll be in a dark place, behind iron doors and bars. You'll walk in a concrete yard. You'll never be free again, for the doctors know you. They won't dare let you free, to kill. There isn't any cure for you, and they understand that."

Astonishingly, the boy began to cry, but his tears and his sobs only made his face appear more wicked and more terrible. He beat the stone on the top of the fence, frenziedly. "I hate you!" he screamed. "I remember when you hit me when I was little, just because I wet myself! I hate your ugly face, I hate the sight of you! If you hadn't come on Friday night you wouldn't be hanging there, and this wouldn't have happened, and you wouldn't have found Petti! It's all your fault, it's all your fault! It isn't MY fault!"

She had diverted his attention; he laid his head on the fence and gave himself up to convulsions of sobs. Alice closed her eyes and prayed for a little extra strength. She had one chance, and one only. She looked up at the strong but narrow stake, which her right hand, now so swollen and red and purpling, clutched so desperately. Then she swung the belt up, holding it by the buckle. The belt curled about the stake, and she sobbed in thanksgiving. She pushed up on the stiff leather, and the end dropped down toward her. Now, with the fingers of her left hand she must clasp the ends together, and somehow, with the help of God, get her head, and then her neck and then her shoulders through the large loop. One slight error, and she would hang herself, and that would be even more frightful than falling to her death below.

She saw the dark-red curls and the round head pressed against the fence; she heard the boy's mingled screams and sobs, and his incoherent exclamations of hatred. Very, very carefully, she joined the ends; it was torture. Her fingers were wet and slippery. But finally, after an eternity of moments, the belt was clasped.

Now, he must not see. She called up to him. "Run away, quick! If they catch you here, they'll know! Run, Angelo, run!"

His eyes, blurred and almost sightless with tears, stared down at her. Then he was gone, and she could hear his running feet on the grass. She cried aloud, "Thank you, Father!" The stone he had dropped fell into the gulf below her, and she heard its dull crash on the rocks.

She carefully tested the belt. Yes, it was strong. But she must not completely trust it. It must be only an aid to her right arm, to relieve some of the tormenting drag on it. She thrust her left arm through it; her body wheeled slightly, and her right fingers slipped on the stake, and encountered the edge of a sharp rock in the soil. She hardly felt it; she concentrated on what she must do. Her elbow rested in the loop of the belt; the leather squealed slightly on the stake. Then she lifted her body upwards as much as possible and dug her toes into the earth of the bluff. It gave her the slightest of purchases. She pressed her body close to the surface of the bluff; inch by inch now, she pushed her arm through the loop; now the leather was under her armpit. She was blinded by sweat and agony. She was forced to rest; the leather, which seemed like a kind and sentient thing to her, engrossed in helping her, gripped at the soft underflesh of her arm. The torture in her right arm faded slightly.

Then she knew that she could do no more; she would have to remain like this until help came; she leaned on the looped belt. It helped her; she could now grasp the stake with her left hand, also. She longed most terribly to loosen her right fingers, but dared not do so; she needed all the aid, the frail aid, at her disposal.

Birds flew above her head, looking down at her inquisitively. The sun burned her eyes; her hair was as wet as though it had been dipped in water. Rivers of sweat ran down her body; she was slimy with it. There was not a muscle anywhere that was not torn with anguish. Drops of blood dripped from the deep cut on her right hand; they slowly wound down her arm.

She became dizzily nauseated; her head was a globe of flame; her heart struggled in her breast and her lungs labored. One foot slipped out of its tiny aperture; she had been leaning too heavily on it for an instant, and her right fingers moved on the stake. But the belt held her under the left arm, and the left hand clutched at the wood. How long, God, she prayed, how long?

Who was screaming? The noise sounded hollow and very far away, in a gathering darkness. The screaming was repeated over and over. And now there were shouts. Mark was shouting, calling! Dear Mark was here at last! She did not know she was screaming also, wild peal after peal, hoarse and panting. She heard, somewhere, the shrieks of a woman, and then other shrieks, also feminine. And then there were running and pounding feet. Through her sweat and tears Alice looked upwards into Mark's white face and horrified eyes.

"Allie, Allie!" he cried. "Hold on, Allie!"

He leaned far over the fence, as far as he dared. He grasped the hands on the stake. She saw his fingers in a terribly clarified light, his brown strong fingers. They moved downward to her wrists, and clutched them. Now he was lifting her slowly; she could see his muscles swell under the thin light cloth of his coat; he was intent on only one thing; his eyes were fixed and unblinking.

Inch by inch, for he was at a disadvantage, and Alice was not a slight girl, he pulled her up; her cheek brushed harshly against soil and the sharp edges of little rocks. Then her eyes were on the level with the first log.

"Can you help a little, Allie?" Mark grunted. "Just a little? When I get your knees to the level of the edge of the bluff, will you lean on it, bending your legs?"

She nodded; she was beyond speaking. But then there was the belt, and Mark uttered a furious cry. It was impeding him, just as it had saved her.

"Grab the stake with your right hand again," he said. "That's right, higher up. Now I'll have to let that hand go. Hold on!" He tightened his grip with one hand on her left wrist, and used the other hand to unfasten the strap. It fell. He seized her right hand once more and pulled her up. She gave no thought to anything now but obeying him; when her knees reached the tearing and crumbling edge of the bluff she thrust them into the soil. Now her head was on the level with the log below the top one. Her face was close to Mark's; they looked into each other's eyes. He smiled. "Good Allie," he said. "Brave, dear Allie."

Then Kathy appeared at the fence, deathly pale, and Mamie. Kathy reached over and grasped her sister's hair; Mamie seized her under the right armpit. That was all she remembered clearly about her rescue.

She was standing in safety now, in Mark's arms, sobbing desperately on his shoulder, clutching him. Then her knees bent under her and she fainted for the first time in her life.

CHAPTER EIGHT

Alice lay in peace in Kathy's pretty rustic bedroom. Her right arm was in a plaster cast, for all the ligaments were torn, the muscles wrenched. She had slept. She had been given a sedative by the doctor. But now she was awake in the twilight and Mark was alone with her, sitting by the bed.

She watched him a moment or two through her lashes. He looked old and weary, and his face was gray and spent, the cheeks fallen in. He was smoking and staring at nothingness.

He knows something! was Alice's first coherent and agonized thought. He suspects something! But he mustn't know, he mustn't suspect. She let herself moan a little, and moved her head, as if awakening. Instantly, his hand was on her forehead. "It's all right, Allie," he said quietly. "You're safe, Allie. Just rest."

Her arm throbbed with fire; the shoulder ached like death itself. She whispered weakly, "Where's—Bruce?"

"The doctor gave him a sedative, too," he replied, and stroked her damp hair. It had an ashen gleam in the twilight. And now he bent over her and looked into her eyes. "Tell me about it, Allie."

"Didn't Bruce tell you?" she said feebly. "It seems all confused to me."

He spoke without any emphasis or emotion, and he watched her. "He said you were sitting on the fence, and that was a damn fool thing to do, Allie, and he was on the porch, and then the next minute you had lost your balance and you fell over. He—he said he tried to help you, but couldn't."

Mark paused. His eyes were closer to hers; she could

not shut her own; his gaze held her and she could not turn away from it.

"He said he tried, and then you told him to go and call the police." Mark paused. He said flatly, "And he did. He was at the telephone just as we pulled into the drive. He was hysterical. The police arrived as you fainted. They stayed around for a little while. Don't you remember talking to Chief Hanley?"

But, terrified, Alice could not remember. She had a vague memory of strange faces floating about her in a shifting pattern of light and shadow. What had she said? She moved her head in assent, and watched Mark with distended eyes.

"You told him the same thing; you said Bruce tried to help, but he was too small to reach you. And then you sent him to telephone—for the police."

Alice gave a great, sinking sigh.

"The only thing," said Mark, in a strange and awful voice, "is that the doctor said that from your injuries he would judge you'd been hanging there for a considerable time, and not for about five or ten minutes. If Bruce had called the police just as we got home, after you had sent him away, right after you fell, the time element would not have been long enough to hurt you like this. The blood was crusted on your arm; your wrist was enormously swollen and purple. That takes much longer than a few minutes, Allie." He paused. "Are you going to tell me the truth, dear?"

But the truth will kill your heart, thought Alice. She tried to smile. "It was just as—we—told you."

Mark slowly shook his head from side to side. He looked at the floor between his knees. "I don't believe you, Allie," he said, and her heart jumped. "Do you know what I think? I think that you fell over that fence at least half an hour before we and the police came. I think that Bruce saw you fall, and heard you scream; I think he—I think he lost his head, and that when you sent him away he hid himself in his room. He does that often, when he's confronted with an emergency. I can't forgive him, Allie. He's a bright boy; he should have known better. If he'd called the police immediately, they'd have rescued you long before we arrived. Am I right, Allie?"

"I—it was so awful; I don't remember just how long—" Alice whispered. The relief made her feel sick and faint again. "But I don't think it was half an hour; perhaps only a quarter, if that long. Don't blame Bruce too much, Mark. He's only a little fellow, after all." Her words were slow and painful. "Just because he's so—intelligent—we forget his age. We expect his actions to match his mind. Children—aren't like that. They grow—kind of lopsided, even the most intelligent."

But Mark was silent. He was still staring at the floor, and then he lifted his eyes and she saw, even in the dusk, that some horror lay at the bottom of them, some fearful suspicion. She forced herself to look at him steadily; her white lips were stiff and unmoving.

"Allie," he said, and his voice was hoarse. "Tell me the truth. After you fell—do you think Bruce deliberately ran away, and waited as long as he could before calling the police?"

"How can you think that?" she cried, and sat up in spite of the blaze of pain in her arm. "It wasn't that way at all! Why should he do that?"

Truth rang in her voice, but it was not the truth he understood.

He wiped his face with his palms, and sighed. "Bruce doesn't like you, Allie. Wait. Let me finish. I've known for a long time that he didn't, ever since the day he smashed the things in your purse. Don't you see I've got to know the truth about this, for Bruce's sake? I've got to know if, after he saw you fall, and heard your scream, that he thought that was the end of you, even though he came running to the bluff where he never usually goes. And then he saw you hanging, and you told him to go to the police, and he—he waited, hoping you'd have to let go. And die. Allie, if that is so, then he attempted to—"

The frightful word hung between them, unspoken. Then Alice shook her head. "It wasn't that way, Mark. You know I don't lie. But I swear to you, in the name of God, that it wasn't as you say. I swear to you."

They looked at each other in another silence. Then Mark sighed once more, and smiled faintly. His forehead was wet. "I believe you, Allie. If—it was as I thought originally, I don't know how I'd stand it. My son. I'd know, then, that he was sick, sick beyond any help."

Kathy opened the door and came in. She was still very shaken. She ran to Alice, put her arms about her sister, and burst into tears. "Oh, my God!" she sobbed. "Oh, my little sister! Oh, what would have happened if we hadn't come home then? Oh, and my poor little boy! He'll never forget this. He'll have nightmares! Oh, you poor children!"

"How is Bruce?" asked Alice faintly, feeling her sister's tears on her face, and attempting awkwardly to pat her back with her left hand. "Hush, Kathy dear. How is Bruce?"

Kathy sat down on the edge of the bed; she clutched Alice's left hand tightly. She sobbed with helplessness. "I don't know! He woke up an hour ago, and I brought him his tray, and then he cried and couldn't stop. I had to feed him like a baby, and then I had to rock him in the rocker until he fell asleep again. And Alicia! Do you know what he asked me to do? He asked me to find out how you were, just before he fell asleep, and he sent you his very best love!" Kathy wept again. "Doesn't that break your heart?"

Alice leaned against her sister and closed her eyes, and the nausea was a great and swelling lump in her throat. "It's all right," she murmured thickly. "Please, Kathy dear, don't cry so. It's all right. Everything will be all right."

It was very early the next morning when Mamie came into the bedroom with the breakfast tray for Alice. But Kathy was already bathed, and out of the room. She had promised Angelo to get him some of the red raspberries he particularly loved, and she had gone down to the village, "to get them early and sweet and fresh, before they've been handled by others." Mark was still sleeping in exhaustion on his couch in the living room. Mamie put the tray beside Alice's bed, and smiled at her encouragingly. "Want me to feed you, Miss Knowles? My, that was an awful day, yesterday, wasn't it?"

"I can feed myself, thanks," said Alice, with a grateful smile. "I'm ambidextrous, you know. That means I can use each hand equally well. Yes, it was a bad day."

Mamie looked about the room cautiously. Then she

tiptoed to the door, opened it and glanced at the sleeping Mark at the end of the living room. She came back to the bed and her pleasant face was stern.

"Mrs. Saint said you insisted you would leave this morning, and that Mr. Saint would drive you into the city," she said. "And Mrs. Saint says that's nonsense, with your cast and all, and you'll be here for a week or more, until you can use your right arm."

She paused. Alice shook her head, and drank the orange juice. "No, I must go back, I really must, just as soon as I've finished this good breakfast and can get dressed. Will you help me, Mamie?"

"You mean, you'll leave before Mrs. Saint gets back?" The woman's eyes were inscrutable. "She says she won't be here until about lunchtime. She's shopping in the village."

"I'll have to leave, I'm afraid," said Alice, making her voice sound regretful. She could not stay here and see Angelo again. She asked about the boy. "Oh, he's still asleep. Doped up." At the curious sound in Mamie's tone Alice looked up alertly. Mamie's mouth had taken on a hard line. She began to whisper.

"They don't fool me any, Miss Knowles. I can put two and two together. You know what I think? I think you were sitting on that fence and he pushed you over! He wanted to kill you!"

Alice put down her glass; her hand was trembling. She began to speak, but Mamie interrupted her almost fiercely. "I can see by your face! And I saw his face, yesterday, when we pulled you up." She crossed herself, with simple honesty. "I can tell a murderer when I see one, and he ain't no kid. He ain't a kid at all, Miss Knowles! I've lived sixty years, and I know people. I've watched him for two months. I've stayed just because of Mr. Saint, who's really a saint, in a kind of way. A foolish way." She tried to smile, and her mouth quivered.

"You mustn't—" said Alice, and looked at Mamie with terror.

"Oh, I won't say anything to Mr. Saint." She regarded Alice wisely. "You're an awful good girl, Miss Knowles. One of the best I ever saw. Don't ever be around that kid again; you'll never know what he'll do. Do you know something else? I think he killed that poor little dog, just because he was treating it rough, and it bit him."

Alice stared at the breakfast tray emptily; she had no strength for denials.

"And that's why, when you go this morning, I'm going with you," said Mamie grimly. "I'm already packed. I'll tell Mr. Saint. I won't wait until *she* gets back. I'm afraid, now, to stay here myself. The kid can sort of read minds; he looks at you and it's like mind-reading. And if he gets onto what I know about him, about yesterday and the dog, why, he might stick a knife in my back or something!"

Alice tried to laugh. "Oh, Mamie!"

Mamie shook her head with vehemence. "Miss Knowles," and she lifted a solemn finger. "I don't think it's right not to tell Mr. Saint. Maybe there's a hospital they can put that boy in; he's a devil. Maybe they can cure him."

Alice could not keep from saying, "No, he can't be cured. He was born that way." Her heart was shaking in dread. "The psychiatrists have a name for him. I know a young psychiatrist in the city; we're friends. He's not as dogmatic and ridiculous as some of the others. He told me once—and he never knew Bruce but described his kind to me—that the only thing to do with children like Bruce is to take them to a large city and abandon them in a crowd, and never see them again! But, of course, you can't do that. You can't even put them in hospitals, for they aren't insane, not legally, not insane as the law regards it. You see, Bruce is a psychopath."

"Words!" said Mamie, shaking her head. "I just say they're devils." She heaved a gusty sigh. "And kids like that boy grow up, and then they murder people."

"Not always," said Alice sadly. "Not very often, I think. But they create misery and unhappiness among others. Deliberately."

"And you can't whale the devil out of them, when they're little, and change them?"

"No, Mamie. You can't change them. But the time will have to come when they'll be recognized, and then—"

"Then what?"

"I don't know, Mamie! I don't know! We don't even know what percentage of such children are born! Sometimes not even psychiatrists can recognize them, for they're often very clever and very intelligent. You can only tell by looking at their families, and seeing how wretched they are that there is one among them, a husband, perhaps, or a wife, or a child. You see, Mamie, conscience is a new development in mankind. At one time, before the rise of civilizations, men had no more conscience than other animals; they were what we call primitives. And psychopaths, as that doctor told me, are resurgences of primitiveness, throwbacks as far as a lack of a conscience is concerned. It's like being born color-blind, which is another form of primitiveness."

"Dear God," breathed Mamie. "Well, anyway, Miss Knowles, I'm leaving with you."

Alice was glad of this, though sorry for Kathy. There would be, then, no private, no dangerous conversation with Mark in his car when he drove her back to the City.

Alice and Dr. John McDowell sat and smoked cigarettes after the excellent dinner they had had at the Tavern near the Parkway. The Tavern stood at a height, and looked down at the running river of lights going to and from the City. Alice felt drained; she smoked and sipped listlessly at her brandy, and glanced about the large rustic room in which she and her friend sat, and wondered, dimly, how so many people could be happy and full of laughter and without any sign of unhappiness in their faces. After following her wandering gaze, the doctor looked at her with affectionate curiosity, and yet he was very anxious and disturbed. He was very subtle, and he said, "Don't let their faces deceive you, Alice. They're probably as wretched and frightened as you are, many of them. No one could tell, looking at you, that you were upset."

Alice, in her dark-blue linen suit, and her small blue hat, looked very beautiful, the doctor thought, for he loved her and wanted to marry her. He glanced down at her right wrist; the cast had been removed two weeks ago, but the wrist was still discolored and swollen. Alice had told him the long and terrible story while they ate dinner, and he had listened in silence.

"There are things you have to accept, no matter how

horrifying," he said. "They're part of reality, Alice. If you'd told me about that boy earlier, informing me he was your nephew and that you hated each other, I'd have warned you to keep a big distance between you. Now, don't jump to conclusions; you're thinking of other children like him, and there may be millions—we don't know—in the world, and being born every day. It's a rare intelligent psychopath who commits murder, for they love themselves too much and want to protect themselves. When they do commit murder, it's after long, cool months, and perhaps even years, of consideration and weighing the dangers. I think that most unsolved murders are committed by intelligent psychopaths. The stupid psychopaths are usually petty criminals, or drug addicts. There is one thing about the intelligent ones: they very rarely commit crimes impulsively, and that's why the law makes a distinction between those who kill on furious impulse and those who premediate murder. The boy has been thinking of destroying you for a long time."

He smiled at her, but she regarded him gravely. "So, keep away from him. I'm sorry, for my own sake, that you're going to Boston, but I can understand." Now he stopped smiling. "And I can have some hope, then, that you'll forget Mark Saint and begin to think about me."

But Alice said, "And there's no hope for Angelo? Shock treatment, or something?"

"No. Except reducing him to a sort of vegetable existence through lobotomy. And that would be as terrible as the way he is now. Cheer up, Alice. I know half a dozen brilliant and successful and respected men, in the professions and in business, who are psychopaths. As far as any of their friends know, they've never committed a crime in their lives, and it's possible they never did, and never will. Angel is now about to enter another stage in his development: he will have to pretend to have a real conscience —and he must make many friends. You'd be surprised to discover how many devoted friends psychopaths have! So, within a few months, perhaps a year, you'll see a change in him. He will imitate all the virtues of others, for his own purposes. Virtue rises out of conscience; psychopaths have no conscience, but they watch and see what is socially desirable and approved, and then they do it. They normally have uncontrollable fits of passion; they learn to restrain themselves among strangers and friends, and give way to their rages only when safe among their husbands and wives, who won't betray them. They are violent, but to strangers they appear the most agreeable and affectionate and cooperative and helpful people in the world, and only among their families do they become tigers of greed and cruelty. They appear absolutely lovable, but they are incapable of selfless love, just as they are incapable of respecting virtue and goodness. All these are civilized attributes, and the psychopath, as I've told you, is absolutely uncivilized in the nobler meaning of the term, 'civilized.' "

"Yes," said Alice. "You once told me they were the best of imitators, for their own purposes. You think, then, that Angelo won't try anything violent again?"

The doctor looked at her hopeful face, and hesitated. "I don't know, Alice. You see, he knows he can't deceive you, and that's why he hates you. His parents are safe—unless," and his voice dropped, "one or both of them catch on to him. And even then, and don't look so frightened, he won't use violence against them because he needs them to support and protect and cherish him. His father means money for his comfort; his mother means adoration and service. And within a little while he'll realize that it will be for his good not to show hostility or hatred or violence even toward those who suspect him. He will begin to learn about law, which could threaten, imprison and destroy him. And, to live, the psychopath needs the affection, assistance and loyalty of others, whom he can exploit."

"What's bred in the spirit is born in the flesh," murmured Alice.

"Yes. We don't know whether the psychopath is developed by way of a sudden mutation of genes in the embryo, or whether he is a true throwback."

"Would you say the Russian people are atavists, throwbacks?" asked Alice.

The doctor smiled, and shook his head. "No. Otherwise the Soviet concentration camps would not exist; they'd all be psychopaths, and serve what would advance them through conformity. But secret observations, and reports, have shown that conscience is as inbred just as much among the Russian people as it is among any other people. However, their leaders are true psychopaths. Hitler was one; Stalin and Lenin and Khrushchev were others. You will notice that these men hated goodness and virtue and kindness and religion. Above all, religion, which is the nurturer and guardian of man's inborn conscience, which the psychopaths despise; they think those who are restrained by conscience are fools. They honestly believe that."

Alice sighed. "Now that I've introduced you to Mark and Kathy, and Mark is already very fond of you, you'll keep track of things for me, and let me know, Jack?"

"Yes, dear. I've met the boy, too. After I talked with him a few minutes I saw that he is the very prototype of the psychopath. And I wouldn't be the least surprised if he grew up to be a very successful and very loved man, active in community causes, even a pillar of the church. The only ones who will really know about him will be the unfortunate woman he will marry, and perhaps his children. By that time, he wouldn't try to destroy them for knowing, as he tried to do to you. That would injure him, you see. By the way, psychopaths, unless they are restrained by the moral disapproval of the community, which could ruin them, are chronic divorcers, or the chronic divorced. You'll notice that each of their subsequent marriages leads to more money or a better position."

Alice was silent, and her friend knew she was thinking with aching yearning of Mark Saint. He said humorously, "Now, if you married me, Alice, we could adopt Kennie Richards, and give him a real home."

Alice laughed faintly. "That's a real inducement! No, Jack. I'm awfully fond of you, and if I didn't love Mark I'd love you. But it wouldn't be fair to marry you under the circumstances. Besides"—and she faltered—"perhaps we'd give birth to a psychopath as Kathy did."

"The chance of that is two million to one," said the doctor. "It's not an inherited trait; it's a sport. It could happen to any parents. It doesn't 'happen in families,' as the homely term is. It's true that when a psychopath is in a family the other members frequently become neurotic because of strain and suffering and anxiety. But removed from the presence of the psychopath, they regain their mental health and become normal again. When we find a neurotic, in our profession, who is in a state of awful anxiety and who is suffering a psychosomatic illness, we look discreetly to see if he is living with a psychopath, or working for one. Unfortunately, it very often happens that a normal and healthy child is born to a psychopath, and is so injured in his mind and spirit and emotions in consequence that he never recovers his full health and zest in life. I've investigated a few neurotic suicides, and I differ with my colleagues about the causes of many. I've found that in quite a number of cases the neurotic has been driven, in despair, to killing himself because he could not free himself from a psychopath, either because he loved him or was responsible for him, or couldn't escape from him, or the memory of him or her."

"We couldn't round them up, even while they're still children?"

"No. And that would be dangerous; too many neurotic children, suffering from a psychopathic father or mother at home, would superficially show traits of psychopaths and would be branded by people who were not fully capable of finding out the truth. The only thing we can do, if cursed with them, is to get away from them as fast as possible, if adults. If children, we can teach them early to conform to civilized mores, for their own good. And they're so lovingly self-protective that they understand!"

"Would you say that all the inmates in prisons were psychopaths?"

"On the contrary! I'd say very few were. They know how to disguise themselves; they never impulsively put themselves in danger, even the dullest of them. The crimes they commit, when they do commit crimes, are secret, and well thought out. The great crime they commit against others is spiritual. Except when they're children, as in the case of your nephew. The value in detecting them early is to show them that open violence will destory them themselves, and that to profit they must imitate virtue. And you can never restrain them through religion, or change them through religion, for what religion could work on is absent in them. But they are frequently supporters of churches; that's part of their disguise."

"Poor Kathy. Poor Mark," sighed Alice, almost crying.

"Oh, don't say that. Your sister will probably never find out about her son, unless, if she ever becomes a widow, she lets him take away her money from her. He'll probably even make her very proud, as a man—if she's discreet about her money and keeps it. He'll be the most affectionate of sons to his mother. As for Mark," and the doctor brooded, "I'm afraid he's already found out to some extent. But there's nothing we can do about it. There's not a mental hospital anywhere who'd take Angelo in. All the tests would show he was eminently sane. And he is. Much more sane than the neurotics he'll create later when he has a family of his own."

Alice gathered up her gloves; her face was pale and strained. She could not forget the terror of that day in the summer when she had almost been murdered. At night her wrist frequently woke her with pain; quite often she had nightmares when the scene was reproduced in a monstrous light.

"I just hope," she said, "that there won't be any psychopaths among the children I'll be teaching in that private school!" She tried to laugh.

"If there are, you probably won't recognize them. But if you find a chronic liar, who has no reason to lie out of fear of a parent, or any other severe person, or an unusually cruel and smiling child, and one who has coaxing and charming ways with adults, who usually adore him or her for his or her brightness or beauty or charm, then you can have your suspicions, but only your suspicions. You can't really be sure."

Alice looked down at her gloved hands. "Do you think, Jack, that Kathy is partly at fault? Do you think if Angelo had a less adoring mother it might have been better for him?"

"Well. Worshiping parents are a danger, for they sharpen the dangerous traits of born psychopaths. However, strong discipline wouldn't help, either; it only makes the psychopath more vengeful, more sly, more secret. Heighho! And who could be so heartless as to tell a fond mother that her son was a curse to humanity? And that she could not appeal to conscience to restrain him, but only to his self-interest?"

Alice colored a little, for religion was too sacred to her to talk too freely of it. "Do you think, perhaps, Jack, that psychopaths are born without souls?"

He was silent for several moments, and then he said frankly, "I know this is unorthodox, and would be laughed at by other psychiatrists, but I honestly think that is it. Or, as I am a Catholic, I would say that from the moment of their conception they were possessed by evil."

Before they left the Tavern, Alice said, "You'll take care of Kennie Richards, Jack? You'll watch him for me?"

"Of course, dear. I love the boy, too. And beginning next Sunday I'll take him to Sunday school. And take him on excursions as you did."

They went out into the warm early September night, full of spicy odors which could lift the spirit. But Alice was beyond stimulation and joy now. Mark Saint stood in her mind even when she was not actively thinking of him. Perhaps she would never see him again. She hoped she would not, for now she knew that he loved her as she loved him, and there was Kathy whose wifehood must not be endangered, whose marriage must not be destroyed.

CHAPTER NINE

Mark Saint was helping his wife to decorate what she coyly called, "Angel's own special little tree!" It was not enough that the family had a large Christmas tree in the living room; Angelo must have a small one in his bedroom so he would not get his feet chilled in the early morning when he left his bed to examine his lavish gifts. The boy stood off at a little distance, critically examining his parents' efforts. Sometimes he shouted angrily, and relocated a globe or an ornament. He was nine years old, but it was not expected of him (and he did not desire it anyway) to lend any assistance. "It is our joy!" Kathy would carol. She listened meekly and with a fatuous smile to her son's criticisms.

"Oh, you don't like that little sled there, darling?"

"No! It should be right there, on that branch. And I hate that silly angel on the top of the tree. Why can't you put a star there, instead?"

"That's my angel, son," said Mark, remembering that his boy was "only a child," and trying not to be offended. "My parents bought it for our trees at home when I was younger than you. I think it's very decorative, and, after all, we must remember that Christmas is not only for gifts and pleasure; in fact, it isn't for that at all. It is celebrated in honor of God's birthday."

"Yes, Daddy," said Angelo at once, and with seriousness. "I know that. It's only that the angel looks motheaten. And people use stars, too, you know. And a big star represents Our Lord's birth, just as much as an angel does."

"Oh, isn't he the brightest!" sang Kathy, and ran to hug her son in an ecstasy of delight. "He understands everything! Oh, my darling, my darling Angel! We'll take

93

the angel off, of course. You are so right, my dearest. A nice big glittering star. I have one right here, in the box."

So the angel was replaced by a tinsel star. Kathy peeped at Mark, and said indulgently, "Oh, you can put it on the big tree, Mark, in the living room. Don't be such a baby and look so depressed." It was beyond her to understand Mark's hurt, his feeling that his son had delicately rejected him. Then he returned his wife's smile; Angelo had just turned nine; he was seeing shadows again and he had determined not to watch for them a long time ago. And over a year ago he had given up calling his son Bruce. The pressure had been too strong from both Kathy and the boy. Besides, the children at the private school he attended did not jeer at the "Angel Saint."

Mark, holding the repudiated angel in his hand, looked up at the star and felt some contentment. He did not love Kathy, but what he had had for her had been replaced by tolerant affection, for he now concentrated on her many considerable virtues which, though petty, were comfortable in many ways. And now that Alice was no longer in the City, Kathy had also changed toward him. It was as if some burr had ceased to irritate her flesh, though her affection for her sister was real if shallow. There were moments when she enjoyed her husband's company even without Angelo's presence; there were even moments when she did not speak of her son at all. In the evenings, when the boy was in bed, there were sometimes actually two hours together when she could discuss brightly things that interested Mark. In some subtle and self-protecting way, and through some female instinct, she had come to realize, without putting it in words even to herself, that she had been on the verge of losing her husband entirely. She made many efforts to be to Mark what she had been to him before Angelo's birth, and often succeeded.

Mark said, "What did you send Alice for Christmas, Kathy?"

"Oh, my dear! I told you! You know how old-fashioned Alicia is sometimes; a real old maid, unfortunately. These masculine young girls often turn out that way. Well. She wanted a muff—a muff—to go with that ancient muskrat coat of hers, which we bought her for Christmas five years ago. You remember it?"

"It looked as pretty on Alice as mink," said Mark.

Kathy was not certain she cared for this remark. Angelo slid his eyes to his father and watched him from under his thick lashes. The corners of his cherubic mouth deepened as if with a suppressed and malicious inner smile.

"I thought she would be coming home this Christmas," said Mark, hanging some tinsel on a branch. "Do you realize we haven't seen her since last summer, when Angelo was at camp, and it was almost a year before that that we saw her?"

"She always has excuses," said Kathy. "Frankly, I don't think family bonds and closeness and togetherness mean much to Alicia. I wonder why she never married Dr. McDowell; she hinted once that he was interested in her, but I don't know."

"It wasn't Alice who hinted," said Mark, with obscure annoyance. "It was Jack McDowell who told us himself, a year or less ago."

"Really?" said Kathy vaguely. "I wonder what he saw in her. Oh, she's my sister and I love her, but she certainly isn't very feminine. I tried and tried to get her to overcome her brusque ways and the manly way she has of blurting out disagreeable truths. And how she dresses! Nothing soft and sweet and pretty; everything severe and simple."

Mark thought of Alice; he always wondered why the deep pain in him never diminished but grew stronger with time. Kathy continued, smiling: "I wonder if she knows that her dear Jack is engaged to Mary Whiteside?"

"Mary was her friend; she introduced them! Have you honestly forgotten, Kathy? Don't you remember that it was only last July that Alice wrote to you about the engagement and how happy she was about it?"

"Um," murmured Kathy. She glanced at her son with a gay laugh. "Now we're almost finished! And then we'll go have our nice cup of hot chocolate in the kitchen, and some of that wonderful cake Betty made today! Just think! Day after tomorrow's Christmas, and all the lovely, lovely gifts! Aren't you happy, Angel?"

Then Angelo did something which he knew enraged his father though Mark had never mentioned it. He jumped high in the air like a very little child and clapped his hands and squealed. Kathy stood back, adoring him. Can't she see that he's deliberately mocking her, making fun of her? Mark said to himself. He always does that when she's particularly precious and speaks in that simpering tone of voice. Why can't she realize he's nine years old and isn't an infant any longer? Then Mark saw that Angelo was watching him after that childish outburst and enjoying his shame and anger.

Mark smiled at his son painfully, and Angelo smiled back and winked just a little. Mark did not know whether to be more angry, or to be amused. It was certainly wrong of him to feel a sudden close warmth because his son had drawn him into a masculine amusement against feminine foolishness. But then Mark decided it was not; men often exchanged winks at the expense of their wives, and Mark did not doubt that women had their own secret exchanges at the expense of their husbands.

He decided not to be too introspective, as he often so decided. Let's keep everything simple, he thought. I have a kid who looks three years older than he is, and who is a perfect physical specimen and getting handsomer by the day, and two years ahead of the other kids his age. He eats up the most difficult school material like a wolf. The kids no longer avoid him; the house teems with his friends, and he fascinates them. His teachers respect, admire and love him. Everything's turning out all right! It was just a matter of time, after all. Me and my nightmares! Even Sally and Bobbie run around him at the cabin like two worshiping dogs now. He's a natural leader. It was just a matter of him getting adjusted and out in the world, away from Kathy. Though she screamed and cried for hours about him going to camp, he went with pleasure and came back covered with adulation. And he's slowly growing to be quite a pal of mine, too. He's as sharp as a knife.

"What are you standing there for, in a dream?" asked Kathy. "We're finished; it's almost time for Angel to go to bed and be tucked in and read to for a while. Let's go into the kitchen. I do hope Betty didn't leave the pan on the fire; it gives the chocolate such an ugly skin on top and Angel hates it that way. Oh, dear. Help grows worse by the day."

"Betty?" said Mark. "Hell. They come and go as through a revolving door. I hardly get to know their names before they've whisked themselves off. I thought her name was Anna."

"And you hinted I was forgetful! Why, Betty's been with us five days! But she's already begun to sulk and mutter under her breath. I kept the last replies to my ad, though, and I can always get another."

"The turnover around here!" said Mark. "Your ad? I thought you got all your help from the agencies."

"They're as bad as the girls! They listen to all the lies their applicants tell them about employers. I never told you, but none of the agencies will send us anyone again. What a world we have now! Besides, the agencies want employers to pay the most enormous wages, and Social Security—"

"I believe Social Security is just a matter of a little law," said Mark dryly.

"It's an outrage," said Kathy, brushing off some shreds of tinsel from her billowing, dark-blue skirts. "And really, the kind of women who answer your ads! You remember Bertie, the one we had in October? She left without even giving notice, just stealing away in the night like an Arab, as that poem or something says. And do you know what she told that agency? You wouldn't believe it!" And Kathy burst into a peal of girlish laughter.

"What?" said Mark. He wished Kathy would not strive so desperately to be what someone had called her in her girlhood—"radiant." She was thirty-nine, yet she still made her eyes big and round, and actually could manage to send a beam from her forehead and lips, and would show all her pretty white teeth and throw her body around vivaciously. It must be wearing, was Mark's uncharitable comment to himself. Why doesn't she let herself go and take her age gracefully? For Mark had discovered, inadvertently, his wife's actual age, though he was too kind to let her know.

"Well," said Kathy, and bent youthfully from her waist, and clasped her hands together and pushed them between her knees. She ran the tip of her red tongue over her lips and looked up at Mark with the expression of a girl of fifteen, and a delighted one at that. "Bertie told the agency she'd been poisoned! Poisoned! Right here in this wonderful home of ours! Honestly! I'm not exaggerating, Mark, so don't look so astonished. Did you ever hear anything like that?"

Mark did not know why, but a tiny cold finger touched his heart. "She must have been crazy," he said. He made himself laugh. "Which one was Bertie, and how long did she stay, and what was the matter with her?"

Kathy flung herself with the abandon of a child into the nearest chair. She looked at her son, who was listening avidly, and grinning. "Angel, you shouldn't hear this. It's too stupid, too mad. You aren't old enough to know such things about such dreadful people. Do go downstairs and drink your chocolate; your own special little mug is right there on the kitchen table; I put it there myself. And don't eat too much of that delicious cake!"

"Sure, Mum," responded the boy, in the indulgent voice of a man humoring a child. He left his bedroom and closed the door behind him softly.

"Such a darling," said Kathy, with yearning, after following him with her eyes. "Oh, Bertie. She was the tall thin one, you know, with glasses, and her hair in curls on the top of her head. You remember? Forty-four, she said, though she was at least ten years older."

"I remember now," said Mark. "She was very well educated; she had had two years of college in some small town in Michigan, and took a home science course for a year after that. And she was only forty-four; I paid her Social Security and saw her records. She was the best cook we ever had. Wasn't she with us for two weeks or more?"

"Almost three. I don't care what her Security card said! I can guess women's ages within a year, so don't be petty, Mark. Educated? She was the most stupid of the whole stupid crowd of them. You remember how Angel detested her from the beginning."

Again the cold minute finger touched Mark's heart. "I didn't know," he said slowly. All at once a heaviness came to him and he sat down.

"Well, he did, and no wonder. She wasn't here a day before she showed that she detested The Children. She was a widow, and had a daughter in some cow college somewhere, and how she had a girl that young at her age

I don't know, and she told me distinctly when I hired her that she loved The Children, all children, or I'd never have hired her at all. She was the most awful liar. Angel came home from school—she hadn't seen him before—and I introduced her to him, and he was a perfect little gentleman as always. And then when he'd gone into the kitchen for his after-school snack—I was interviewing her in the breakfast room—she looked at the door he'd gone through with big crazy eyes behind her glasses. I just thought, then, that she was captivated with him, as everyone else is. But she wasn't. She hated him from that very minute, and he hated her, though he never showed it, of course. I ought to have known! Oh, there was never a word between them! You know how courteous Angel is with all the help, even with old Sue who does the laundry, and he never raised his voice to Bertie. He'd even get up and open the door for her when she was carrying a tray or something heavy."

"Please get to the point, Kathy," said Mark. Was it stuffy in the room? It was a little hard to breathe. "What did Bertie tell the agency?"

"I told you! She said she'd been poisoned! The very afternoon of the night she left, creeping out of the house like a thief."

"How?" demanded Mark.

"You don't have to shout, Mark, though I don't blame you. I really don't blame you. You know how sort of pale and thin she was, though she was a good worker, I admit. She kept a bottle of iron-something in the refrigerator, though I didn't like it there—germs. She took three spoonfuls a day, I think. Well, that afternoon was rainy, or I wouldn't have been home; it was the monthly meeting of the Mothers Against Polio. I thought I'd write some letters, and I was at the desk in the living room—I think I was writing to Alicia—when I heard Bertie scream. I thought it was a burglar, or some other kind of criminal, breaking into the house, and my heart jumped right into my throat. I ran into the kitchen, and she was sitting there at the table, her eyes popping right out of her head, and glaring, and then, all at once—the disgusting thing!—she vomited right on the newly washed kitchen floor! And kept right on sitting there, vomiting, clutching the table, though I shook her hard and told her to stop it at once. She did it deliberately, she was so contemptible. And it served her right that the last throw-up was stained with blood, from straining like that and being so hysterical."

Mark said nothing. He thought, dimly, that the room was very hot; his forehead was sweating, and yet the sweat was cold.

"I made her wash up her mess and then go to her room to lie down. When it was time to get dinner she refused to come downstairs. She had locked her door! So I had to get all the dinner myself. Don't you remember? And the next morning she wasn't there, the awful, crazy wretch. And telling that story to the agency, too. That's why they wouldn't send me any other help after that."

"What was the name of the agency?" asked Mark.

"The Acme!"

"I see," said Mark dully. He did not know it was instinct that made him get quickly and noiselessly to his feet and tiptoe, running, to the door and throw it open. Angelo stood there. He smiled at his father. "I guess I'll go to bed now," he said. "I drank my chocolate and ate my cake. I washed out the pan, too."

"Good boy!" cried Kathy, clapping her hands. "And now to beddy-bye. Mark, will you excuse us? Angel and I have something very, very special to talk to each other about, alone, and we don't want you listening!" She peeked up at her husband archly. "After all, it's almost Christmas."

Mark went down to the kitchen, walking very slowly, as if half asleep. He looked at Angelo's mug. It was standing on the sink. Mark put his finger inside it; it had been rinsed out. Stop it, he said to himself. He looked at the big chocolate cake on its decorated plate. A piece had been cut. He looked into the garbage pail, but nothing was there. Then he went into the powder room. He turned on the light and looked about, for what he did not know. But he found a crumb of dark cake on the floor. Angelo had not drunk the chocolate or eaten the cake. He had not had the time. But he had known he must leave some lying evidence that he had drunk and eaten quickly, and after he had he'd stolen upstairs to listen at his door.

"My God," said Mark, in a dull voice. But he did not think of the "mad" Bertie. He was seeing, again, a desperate girl clinging to a wooden stake and hanging over a deadly gulf of air and sunshine.

"No, no, I mustn't start all that again, after over two years of peace," he said. But he knew he must.

Four o'clock the next afternoon Mark Saint was sitting in the sun room of a pleasant home in another suburb, talking with Bertha Symes. The lady of the house had discreetly left, after Mark had identified himself and explained that there was something he wished to ask his former employee. "I hope it isn't anything serious," she had said mildly. "We're very fond of Bertie, and she likes us."

"It's nothing serious," Mark had said, forcing a smile. "It's just that I had some papers at home, some blueprints, and I can't find them. Bertie was always very tidy, and she may have put them away too well."

The Acme Agency had been suspicious, too. And cold to Mark. The woman in charge vehemently insisted not only on Bertie's sanity but on her competence and character. Bertie had been with her "last family" fifteen years before she had gone to the Saints; if the lady hadn't died, she would have been with them still.

"If Bertie said she had been poisoned at your house," said the woman, "then she had. I'd believe anything Bertie said, without a stack of Bibles."

"But it's preposterous!" said Mark. "Who would poison Bertie, and why? This is insane! If she thought that, why didn't she call the police, and a doctor?"

The woman hesitated, and moved a pencil in her fingers. "She did call her doctor and he was out of town. And she said she was afraid to wait downstairs and call another one. She locked her door, and then left that night. But Bertie is very intelligent. She went into your kitchen for her bottle of tonic and it wasn't where she kept it. She looked everywhere. You see, she was going to give it to the police to be examined. After she told me about it, I urged her to go to the police anyway; she was still very weak and sick. But she said she'd thought it over; she liked you, Mr. Saint. She didn't want you to be upset."

The woman looked at him steadily. "Why don't you talk to Bertie herself? I'll give you the address where she is working now. I'm sorry, Mr. Saint. You know, it could be a mistake after all. Perhaps the tonic had gone bad." But her tone was doubtful. She would not say anything more.

Mark had then driven to this house in another suburb, certain he was not awake but dreaming some dreadful dream. And now he was sitting near Bertie and questioning her. She looked at him with large violet eyes in which intelligence and sanity beamed without flaw, and she was very sober and very neat in her white uniform.

"When my doctor came back, Mr. Saint, I did go to him, and he was furious because I hadn't called another doctor immediately, to examine what I'd vomited and take a sample. And I couldn't find my iron tonic anywhere. I know I'd put it back after I had taken a dose after lunch; I had to move a milk bottle so it was out of sight. Mrs. Saint didn't like to see it there. And just before I left—it was after two in the morning—I looked everywhere for it. I even went into the garage and looked into the garbage pails. Mr. Saint"—and her voice dropped—"I'm glad now that I didn't find it, that it was earlier taken away and destroyed."

A silence like a malignant presence stood between them. Mark had to make a physical effort to break it, finally.

"Why, Bertie? Why are you glad you couldn't find the bottle for the police?"

"Mr. Saint, I'd rather not talk about it anymore. Suppose we just leave it like this."

"No, Bertie, we can't. I've got to know. Who was in the house that day?"

"No one but Mrs. Saint and I." Then, "Please, Mr. Saint, I have a roast in the stove." But he caught her wrist, gently, as she tried to rise. "What did the doctor think might have been in your tonic, Bertie?"

She answered, reluctantly, "He thought it might have been arsenic." She hesitated. "You know, while I was in the garage, looking into the pails, I saw that rat killer on the shelf. It said it contained arsenic, and was poisonous." She waited a moment, then went on, "I forgot my tonic after breakfast. I took it after a big lunch. The doctor said that that saved my life, probably. And my vomiting. I have a very sensitive stomach. I vomit very easily."

It was all shadowy, unsubstantial. "I vomit very easily." Mark could breathe with a little less difficulty now. "Didn't you notice any wrong taste, Bertie?"

"I thought I did. I thought the medicine was a little gritty, too. But when it's down that low the ingredients, some of them, sometimes precipitate. It was two-thirds gone."

"It could have spoiled, Bertie. Those tonics sometimes do."

"Yes, yes," she said, with too much eagerness, her pitying eyes on his face. "That must be it. In fact, the next day I thought of it myself, and that is why I didn't go to the police. It would have been so embarrassing for you, and you were always so kind to me, Mr. Saint, and so generous. And I had no proof at all."

Mark twisted his hat in his hands and looked at it. "Bertie, how did you get along with Angelo?"

Again the malignant silence stood between them. Then Bertie said, honestly, "We never said much to each other, Mr. Saint. I like children, I really do. I like them around; I wouldn't work where there were no children; I raised the children of my last family. But, somehow, Angelo and I didn't hit it off at all. He was always polite to me. Perhaps I'm getting a little impatient, but I'd snap at him once or twice for suddenly appearing right behind me in the kitchen, without making a sound. And he'd just laugh. He'd just laugh." Her face was eloquent.

"You didn't like each other." Mark's voice was without inflection.

"You can put it that way if you like, Mr. Saint. You know how it is; you sometimes look at a stranger and dislike him at sight. I'm afraid that was the way between Angelo and me. At first, I was ashamed for—disliking—a little boy. And then I began to think he wasn't a little boy at all. Now, isn't that silly?"

"Everyone else seems to love my son," said Mark with an effort. "But you didn't."

"No, Mr. Saint. I didn't. Please don't ask me why. And now, I've really got to look at that roast."

Mark went home, driving slowly in a fine sleet, and in

the early darkness. He went directly to the kitchen where Betty was alone, preparing dinner. She gave him a look of pleasant greeting. She was young and red-cheeked, with blonde hair.

They chaffed each other for a moment, then Mark said idly, "Betty, I hope you'll stay with us. We like you very much. I hope you like us."

Her face clouded a little. "Well, Mr. Saint, you know I'm not supposed to do a lot of things that I do. But I like you all. And I love Angelo. He's a darling."

So, thought Mark, Betty is safe. And he was struck with terror that he could think this, and he wondered if he were losing his mind.

CHAPTER TEN

"Well," said Kathy, one spring evening over a year later, "it's wonderful the way you show so much interest in your child, considering that other fathers don't, always, but you look so tired, Mark, and perhaps you'd better not go to the spring party at the school tonight. Come to think of it, I'm not feeling so chipper myself lately."

Her doctor had told her frankly, yesterday, that her symptoms were probably those of the menopause, for she did not lie about her age to him. But she had been annoyed. Here she was, only forty, and the fool thought just over forty middle-aged! He was getting senile. She would have to think about going to that nice Dr. Hauser all the girls loved so much. It had been a very gay and strenuous winter, and she had done a lot of entertaining— she was famous for her parties and dinners. Her feeling of heaviness, her sour stomach, her sudden sweats, her occasional nausea, were just the results of a season that had been more active than usual. But she looked at Mark with affectionate concern. He was very thin; he had never been overweight, but now he was positively emaciated! Why hadn't she noticed it before? And the shadows under his eyes were a deep gray, and his skin looked unhealthy. She was alarmed, not only because she loved him as much as she could, but because Angelo needed him.

"Did you go to the doctor?" asked Mark. "You said you were going."

"Oh, Dr. Bowes!" cried Kathy airily. "You know how he is. He dismisses everything unless you have TB or cancer or diabetes or a broken leg. He isn't interested in anything else but those."

She was rapidly working herself up to what Mark was beginning to call her "Katherine mood," bubbling, effervescent, radiant, with a fixed bright stare and a fixed bright smile. Her voice was already taking on the "Katherine" sound, murmurous, effusive, and sympathetic. Did she practice it just before emerging in public? Mark asked himself, and hated himself for the uncharitable question. He remembered that when he was going with her before marriage she was like this; a month or two of marriage had brought out her real nature, which was practical, avaricious, cynical, and pragmatic. Though she was only talking with him here in the house, the mood was absorbing her; in her mind's eye she was meeting Angelo's teachers and impressing them with her profound sweetness, her eagerness to understand their problems, her anxious, smiling willingness to be informed. Oh, Kathy, thought Mark, with tiredness. It must be a heavy burden now for you to pretend to the vivacity of youth, the abundant spirits of youth, the hopefulness of youth. Why can't you relax and be the middle-aged woman you are? No one expects a woman of your age to be enthused and buoyant. I'm sorry. You were too old, at thirty, to have your first child. I should have insisted that we have a child when you were still young, so that now, when you are in the company of women much younger than yourself with children Angelo's age, you would not be at such an exhausting disadvantage. You are not young, Kathy; many women of your age are grandmothers. Your son should be in college now, seriously concerned with the profession he will follow in a year or two; you should not be the mother of a young boy.

Kathy was dressed in a beautiful spring outfit, consisting of a light blue silk dress with the usual swirling skirts which concealed her swelling buttocks and massive legs. But fine lines webbed her delicate face; her hair was still vivid auburn, but Mark suspected this was partly art emanating from her beauty salon. There were gray marks of strain under her blue eyes. At first glance, Kathy appeared young; at second glance, she appeared even older than she was. Her breasts were beginning to have a heavy sag; her throat, never beautiful, was a saffron color now and grooved with lines, and had a twisted look. And her feet were puffed and thick in the dark blue shoes.

Mark, three years younger than Kathy, felt a passionate

regret and sorrow for her, and he did not quite know why. And then it suddenly occurred to him that never, in all their married life, had he asked her what she really thought about their son. In earlier years he had taken it for granted that he knew; but he understood, tonight, that he did not know.

"Kathy," he said, as he put on his coat, "you're with Angelo most of the day, when he comes home from school, and you spend a lot of time at night going over his lessons with him. Kathy, what do you think about Angelo?"

Kathy was combing her auburn curls into a becoming swirl. She paused, the comb in her hand, and regarded her husband with wide eyes in the mirror. "Angel?" she said. "My Angel? What a funny question. He's just my Angel."

She put down her comb, and her face took on its usual ethereal expression when she thought of her son. She clasped her hands on the top of her mirrored dressing table. She began to smile.

"Kathy!" cried Mark, and there was a harsh grating in his voice. "I mean honestly. Not what you think you should think. Not what you believe you should feel. But simply, truthfully."

The smile left her face, leaving it sagging and middle-aged and bleak. "I don't know what you mean! Mark, what's the matter with you? What can I, Angel's mother, think about him, except what others think too, that he's utterly adorable, well-adjusted, brilliant, well-bred, a leader, a boy full of authority and charm? No child could be more delightful than Angel. I thank God every day for being blessed with such a boy, especially when I look at other children his age, so nondescript, so average, so dull, so faceless. Just you wait! Just talk with the headmistress tonight, your great pal, Miss Simmons! She can tell you!"

"I don't care about Miss Simmons." Mark sat down with a feeling of collapse on his bed. "You're his mother. What do you think about him at night, when you're alone, Kathy? Kathy, for God's sake, look at me! I'm your husband; I love you. Angelo's my child, too. Why can't we talk about him without hyperboles? Why can't he be discussed just like any other kid, without extravagance, just soberly and thoughtfully, as other parents discuss their kids?"

Kathy became very quiet. She looked down at her newly manicured nails. "You forget, Mark. Angel's not like other boys."

"In what way?" There was such a constriction in his chest. He looked at the bedroom door. Was Angelo listening there, as he quite often listened?

"He's so superior—"

"Kathy. I'll never ask you again, so help me God, unless you answer me this time, with truth and openness."

"Oh, dear," said Kathy. "You aren't well, are you, Mark? You've been working too hard. Oh, please, don't look so tight! You can be so emotional." She paused, and studied her nails again, and slowly shook her head. "Mark, I don't know. He is so lovely, he's so perfect. Sometimes I wonder if it's right! He should have some faults, I suppose."

"He has them," said Mark grimly. "He has the most awful and uncontrollable temper, flaring up about nothing, and really devastating. You thought it cute when he was younger, when he would angrily sweep the dinner plates and glasses off the table when he flew into one of his rages. He doesn't do that now. I mean, not that childishly. But he becomes uncontrollable, and you know it. He becomes—wild. Almost savage."

"All children have their faults!" said Kathy, coming at once to the rescue of her son. "Angel has his rages; he'll get over them in time. And you know he doesn't go off into them too frequently—hardly once a month now."

"When he did, the last time, you had bruises on your arms, Kathy." Mark's voice was low, but his eyes remained on hers and held them. "Bad bruises."

She laughed prettily. "Oh, he's so strong! He just took hold of my arms and insisted!"

Mark got up and went to his wife and put his hand on her shoulder. She stopped laughing. "Dear," he said, "he's the only child we have. We're responsible for him. Kathy, I think, sometimes, there is something wrong with Angelo, and that perhaps—"

A strange white look of terror swept across her face, wiping away the youthfulness, leaving her features stark.

She flung away Mark's hand. "How can you talk that way! Mark, you must be insane, or something! What in God's name do you mean?"

So, thought Mark, with a taste of sickness in his mouth, she thinks so, too. Perhaps she really doesn't actually think it, but her normal instincts stir, and they frighten her and she puts them out of her mind and consciousness.

Then he said, in a very low voice, "He lies, Kathy. You know he does. He doesn't lie to get out of punishment, or in fear, as normal kids do. He lies without reason."

"That's because he has such an intense imagination!" Kathy's voice fluttered; she clenched her hands on her dressing table. "You know very well, Mark, that all children imagine things; they make up the wildest stories, and actually believe them! Why—don't you remember, when he was four, he shouted that there was a tiger in the garden, a real tiger, with stripes and big teeth, and he really believed it!"

"He isn't four now, Kathy. He's ten. He isn't a baby with an uncontrolled imagination. But he lies. He makes up fantastic stories; he doesn't even expect us to believe them. He lies, and looks us right in the face, grinning and challenging us to refute the lies. You never do. You think it's a sort of 'game,' and you girlishly enter into it with him, and all the time he's making fun of you. Sit down, Kathy, please, and listen to me. This is deadly serious. He is older, mentally and physically, than his age. Why won't you sit down? He isn't deceived by his stories; he isn't just exercising his imagination. He's waiting to see how far he can go, and the further he goes the less he respects you—me."

"You don't understand, Mark! I enter into it, as you call it so meanly, because his stories are so fantastic and so original; he doesn't fool me and he doesn't intend to fool me. It is all such a game, honest it is."

"Such as when he told you that that tiny Miss Jane Whythe, his new English teacher, hates him and persecutes him, and tries to belittle him, and won't let him orate in class as the other children do? And that she torments him? You'll remember that he wanted you to write Miss Simmons and complain about Miss Whythe, who is young and uncertain, and try to get her fired? Do you call that a babyish story?"

"You're making something of nothing! All children dislike some of their teachers and complain about them. It doesn't mean a thing. And I don't care for Jane Whythe much myself. She's hardly more than a mite, and if she weighs eighty pounds soaking wet I'd be surprised. She's trying to compensate for her lack of stature by picking on the tallest and biggest boy in the class, Angel, even if he is at least two years younger than the others."

"Angelo wrote out the letter he wanted you to copy and send to Miss Simmons. It wasn't a child's letter; it was the letter of a vengeful and hating adult."

Kathy's face broke out into a luminous smile. "It was, wasn't it! So mature! Even though I refused to copy it, I had to admire it! You'd think a college boy wrote it!"

But Mark did not smile. He said, "Kathy, please. You've met Miss Whythe. She's anxious and dedicated, and she's only about twenty, and deadly serious about 'her children,' and concerned with them. Do you think she's capable of persecuting any child, and hating any child, or deliberately frustrating any child? Angelo lied, Kathy."

"Well, he doesn't like her. Look at the time! If you're going with me, Mark, we must really go now." Her face was set, and closed to him, and he sighed and stood up and knew it was no use at all. But still he remembered that moment when her face had whitened and looked afraid and stark, and he remembered how her eyes had widened as if she were seeing something frightful which she would not acknowledge even to herself. Love overcame normal instincts of self-preservation and awareness, sometimes to its own destruction. No wonder it preferred to be blind, to accept all things, to endure all things, in order that it might exist, that it might not be dashed into oblivion.

They paused in the breakfast room where Angelo was working on his homework. Betty, with her red cheeks, was contentedly knitting near him, and she smiled at Mark, but not at Kathy. Why she had remained so long was somewhat of a mystery to Mark, except that he had induced Kathy to pay her thirty-five dollars a week to which he surreptitiously added twelve. Yet, he had done the same with others and they had not stayed. She was a very intelligent girl, and she was fond of Angelo, and played games with him, and he repeatedly declared that he liked her, too. Mark believed this. In Betty's comfortable and acquiescent company Angelo was at ease. She demanded nothing from him; she did not ask him to be virtuous, to be kind or considerate, to be honest, to be patient; she did not ask him to love her. Was this the one and only way to deal with people like Angelo, to live with them only on the surface and never to ask of them any love, and responsibility, or any respect? But what do I mean by "people like Angelo"? Mark asked himself. He's not like other kids—what is he like? I think I should see a doctor myself!

Kathy, as usual, began to fuss impatiently as soon as she entered the breakfast room. She was jealous, unconsciously. "Betty, you won't forget Angel's cocoa, will you? Not too much cream; just a little floated on the surface, whipped, with the tiniest smidgen of vanilla—"

"I've been making it every night, Mrs. Saint," said the girl imperturbably. Angelo lifted his incredibly handsome head and grinned at her.

"You don't have to be impudent!" said Kathy sharply. "I was just reminding you. And be sure and take any skin off his rice pudding."

Mark looked at his large and muscular son, who appeared to be at least twelve. "Does he eat every night before he goes to bed?" he asked Kathy.

"Why certainly. He's a growing baby and needs all the nourishment he can absorb," said Kathy, bridling.

The adult and unchildish face now looked smoothly and blandly at Mark. The light brown eyes were as candid as brook water. And all at once Mark thought: He despises me, he laughs at me, he derides me!

The thought was shattering, and it came from nowhere, like a blaze of lightning. Mark took Kathy's arm and said, "Let's go. We're late."

Kathy chattered all the way to the school, where the teachers and parents were to have what Kathy called "their monthly cozy meeting and discussions about The Children." This was a special occasion. The teachers were to entertain the parents not with the usual coffee and little cakes, but a light buffet dinner. The school was a small and private one, and the teachers were unusually capable and well-versed in their subject matter, and the fees were expensive. Mark's plea for a public school had been over-ridden by Kathy. Now he was not displeased; Angelo, in the fifth grade, was studying French and elementary Latin, and the courses were far in advance of the usual public school's. Miss Simmons, the head of this very exclusive school, was independently wealthy, and would accept no boy, no matter what his background or advantages, who was not at least slightly above the average in intelligence. Even then, the dullest fourth were weeded out of the school during the first year, to make room for those more worthy of education. "Let the public schools practice their democracy," she would say with tartness. "But America needs its best minds." She had what she called her "spies" in the neighboring public schools—teachers who reported to her on the superior intelligence of boys in their classes. In some manner, thereafter, these boys would suddenly find themselves in possession of scholarships to Miss Simmons' Boys Academy.

Miss Simmons was a tall and very old lady, but very erect, very commanding, and very thin. Her white hair crowned her head in the style of her youth, and her clear blue eyes had a girllike freshness and directness. Mark thought of her as he was driving through the haunting sweetness and lonely but urgent quiet of the spring evening. She, above all, would never be deceived, not even by a boy as clever as Angelo. He, Mark, would find an opportunity to talk with her alone tonight, tactfully. Unless Kathy tried to monopolize her as usual, with constant eager chatter about her son.

The other parents, already assembled in the special meeting room, greeted Mark in a friendly fashion, but expended their beaming affection on Kathy, who immediately began to trill, to ask, effusively, about The Boys, to listen with sympathy, with birdlike brightness, with gurglings of pleasure, with little soft sounds, with smiles and head-cockings, as the occasions demanded. Mark knew she was not in the least interested in the sons of other parents, that, in fact, she disliked other children and was jealous if they displayed any superiority to Angelo, but she hid this wonderfully well and all were deceived, except her husband. Behind the shine of her intent eyes was a wandering expression which no one discerned; she glanced about her eagerly, to be recognized. She responded to questions about Angelo with a glow. Her billowing skirts kept up a constant little twirl and sway; she clapped her hands lightly, laughed like a child, coquetted innocently, leaned forward not to miss the slightest word. Mark felt so tired that he thought he could lie right there on the polished floor and sleep in spite of the shrill voices and laughter of the mothers, and the subdued chuckles of the fathers. He looked about for Miss Simmons; she was directing the buffet supper over which some of the teachers were so anxious and busy and careful. She began to fill small glasses with sherry. Mark disliked sherry; it gave him heartburn. I could use, he thought, a giant highball, with bourbon, and then I could go to sleep forever. As usual, there were three mothers to every father, and the fathers were yawning and glancing with disfavor, across the room, at the impending sherry. Mark knew only a few of them, and he was in no mood for talk about business or golf or fishing, or even the stock market.

He became aware at last that little Miss Whythe, for whom he had a tender spot as he had for all small young things whether human or animal, was not present. He had met her but once, a shy little creature with dark brown eyes and a mass of lighter brown curls, a pointed, elfin face and a smile that was too serious for her twenty or so years. She was the youngest teacher in the school, and had appeared only last September, and Miss Simmons had remarked that even at her early age she had her master's in English and English literature, and would, next year, have her PhD. Miss Simmons considered her school fortunate to have Miss Whythe on its staff, and, as she herself was old enough, and older, to be the girl's grandmother, she was unusually fond of her.

Mark went over to the table and smiled at Miss Simmons, and her stern, uncompromising face relaxed, and she smiled in return. "How nice to see you, Mr. Saint," she said. She handed him the large sherry bottle; to his regret, he saw it was domestic and not of excellent quality.

But Miss Simmons was not one to spend money lavishly except on her school. He began to help with the pouring of the murky brown liquid. "Not very good," said Miss Simmons cheerfully, "but how many people know a good sherry from a poor one these days? It wasn't like that when I was young, but, ah me! the uses of democracy and what the politicians call 'our constantly expanding and dynamic standard of living'!"

Mark laughed a little. He poured carefully. He said, "Where's Miss Whythe tonight? I particularly wanted to ask her how Angelo is coming along in her class."

"Oh, the poor child. She fell and broke her arm two weeks ago. That doesn't prevent her from coming to class, but she isn't up to parties. Besides, she lives with her old grandmother, and the dear child thinks she mustn't leave the old lady alone in the evenings very often. She supports her, you know. Girls like Jane can't be found very often these days."

"I'm sorry to hear about her arm," said Mark, with true sympathy. "How did it happen?"

"Really, I am sometimes very vexed when I think about it," said Miss Simmons. "She saw all those big boys practicing football and racing and yelling around the schoolyard, and diving and tackling and all the other things they do at that time. They're like wild horses, especially in the spring. I had just had a load of special, porous stones delivered for a rock garden in a spot near the wall where nothing else would grow, and the fool of a man dumped them, not at the spot near the mound of waiting soil, but about fifteen feet away. Jane always takes a shortcut across the schoolyard, to get home faster and catch the bus, but the other teachers are more discreet when they see the bigger boys running and yelling and kicking at practice, or playing baseball. They avoid the schoolyard then and so do the younger children. Of course, it was after four o'clock, and all the other teachers had gone, but Jane had remained behind to talk with a boy." Miss Simmons' face changed subtly. "The boy was leaving the school—at his own request—and he was heartbroken and so was Jane, and she was trying to change his mind.

"Really," continued Miss Simmons, slapping down a

plate, "it was the most stupid thing. I've forbidden the boys to practice so roughly like that at long after four in the afternoon after this, and have put the football team out of bounds for two weeks as a punishment. Poor little Jane was hurrying; she doesn't know, herself, just what happened, except that she was just crossing in front of that big heap of stones, which are odd-shaped and some of which have sharp edges to fit into the soil, when all at once the team stampeded in her direction like wild ponies. The boys weren't looking of course; they didn't see Jane until they were almost on her, and they were pummeling each other, as well as running, and diving at each other's legs, heads bent, and tackling, and heaven knows what else, and shouting like mad. It had been a rainy day, and the light was not very clear. Jane stopped, thinking that the big heap of rocks would give her some protection as she stood in front of them, for naturally the boys would see them and swerve in time. And so they did, barely missing her. But one or two were pounding ahead like mad, wild animals, and they didn't swerve fast enough, and either one or two hurled into Jane. You know, she's so very small, not as tall as many of her own students, and she was just thrown like a feather onto the stones."

"Why, that's bad," said Mark, with honest concern. "And she broke her arm?"

"Fortunately, that was all, and some contusions. Except that her head was hurt, too, but not too seriously. My doctor says that if she hadn't instinctively thrown up her right arm to protect her face and head as she was thrown into the air and then onto the stones, she might very possibly have been killed. As it was, she had to have eight stitches taken in her scalp, slightly above her right ear. But what a brave little thing she is. She was back at school in two days, in spite of my insistence that she remain home for at least a week. Naturally, the school paid her bills, and her income wouldn't have been cut if she had stayed home."

"I hope the boy, or boys, were punished," said Mark, with some anger.

"Oh, you know how boys are. They were all confused. In fact, they didn't know that one or two of them had run into Jane, until they were far back in the schoolyard, and had stopped for breath, and then heard her screaming. They carried her into the school. They were terribly sorry and bewildered; none remembered running into Jane, and I can credit that, considering their boisterousness, and boys' obliviousness in hard play, and the light, and Jane's smallness and her childish weight. They couldn't do enough for Jane; they stayed around until the doctor came, and took turns holding her hand and wiping the blood and tears from her face, and fanning her, for she's a great favorite with them. I believe one or two actually cried, and the others looked like crying. And none could have been kinder and more concerned than your own boy, Angelo."

"Angelo?" Mark carefully put the bottle down, and that infinitesimal cold finger touched his heart.

"Yes. And I was very vexed with Angelo. The boys on the team are all thirteen and fourteen and he had no business practicing with them. Oh, he's a big boy, almost as big as some of them, and a great leader even among the older boys in the last form, and he excels in sports as he does in everything else. Why, only a month ago a delegation of boys"—and she smiled—"who are part of the football team came into my office and begged me to allow Angelo to be with the team, as he is a marvelous tackler, they said. I refused, of course, for, for all his height and strength, he's too young. I expressly told Angelo, in private, that I did not approve of him even practicing with the boys, and he assured me he would not in the future, and would be content with basketball and baseball until he was older. I suppose I'm old-fashioned in this, for I see children of five and six playing football, but I don't approve of younger children on a team with much older and larger boys than they are. It's dangerous."

"And," said Mark faintly, "Angelo was with them that day. Does he—does he—know who ran into Miss Whythe?"

"No. Oh, I shouldn't have mentioned that part of it anyway, Mr. Saint. Angelo is about the most popular, most obedient, most serious, and, perhaps, the most intelligent boy in the school, and this was his first infraction. Please forget about it; he was punished, and now it's forgotten. The boys took up a collection for Miss Whythe to buy her a nice gift, to show her how sorry they were, and . . ."

But Mark was not listening. His gray face was even more ashen than usual. He was thinking of Jane Whythe, who was not even as tall as Angelo, and who weighed much less. He was thinking she might have been killed— Mark wet his lip cautiously with his tongue, as if blood were there, and his lip had a taste of acid on it.

"Does Miss Whythe know who the boy, or boys, were who ran into her?"

Miss Simmons had bent to examine the shrimps Newburg which were bubbling in the chafing dish. From this crouched position she looked up across the table at Mark, and her wide blue eyes were abstracted and a little startled, as if she were surprised to see him still standing there. "I'm sorry," she said. "What did you say, Mr. Saint?"

Mark repeated his question. Did the old lady hesitate a little too long before she straightened up, and, did she linger too long over the dish? Mark did not know that his hands were clenching the lace-covered edge of the table. He did not hear the murmurs and laughter and voices of the others across the room. He saw only Miss Simmons. And now she was gazing at him, sincerely puzzled at his expression and gray pallor.

"Does she know? Mr. Saint, that's a question I've been asking myself for two weeks. Of course, it was an accident, and nothing can undo it. But Jane is such a loving and devoted little thing; she isn't many years older than what she calls 'my boys.' Even if she knew—and I think she knew—she wouldn't tell. I don't blame her, in a way. It was all a stupid accident. All the boys were equally responsible, I suppose, for not watching where they were running, though they all swerved, except that one or two, when they were almost upon Jane. What good would it do, Mr. Saint, for Jane to tell? It would only cause the boy more embarrassment and more wretchedness. And it's very possible that he didn't know himself, in the boisterous excitement. If he had known, he would have stopped immediately, I'm sure, instead of running off with the rest, for everyone loves Jane."

"Of course," said Mark. The cold finger had become a clutch of ice around his heart. "It was an accident."

He said, "Miss Simmons, I'd like to talk with you a moment about Angelo—" But Miss Simmons had lifted a large elephant bell and was shaking it vigorously and nodding and smiling to the parents and teachers across the room.

Mark found Kathy, with a bevy of admiring friends about her. She was, naturally, talking about one of Angelo's latest exploits. He took her arm, and she turned her shining blank eyes upon him and hardly recognized him for a moment. "Kathy," he said, "I've just remembered. I had a flat tire today and left it at the service station three blocks from here. I want to get it before they close in half an hour."

"Why can't it wait until tomorrow?" asked Kathy impatiently. "We're going to have supper now."

Yes, why couldn't it wait? Why couldn't it wait until tomorrow, or, better still, forever? Mark did not know why he should be in such an inner frenzy, and why the terror was now stronger in him than ever before. He only knew that he could not wait, not even for an hour, to know, finally.

"One of the other tires is doubtful," he said. "Look, I'll be back before you know it. Save me some of those shrimps." And he left her, almost running toward the door. I'm out of my mind! he told himself as he found himself in the empty, shining hall and looked about him for the telephone booth he vaguely remembered having seen before. "I'm out of my mind!" he repeated aloud. "What good will it do if I know, or don't know?"

He found the booth; his steps echoed as he ran to it, and he opened the telephone book to look for Jane Whythe's number. Somewhere, dimly, something was crying a prayer that she would not be listed, that a number would not be found in the book. But the name jumped at him from the page, and he fumbled for a coin in wet fingers, dropped the coin in the box and dialed the number. It rang. The prayer changed to a pleading that Jane would not answer, that she would be asleep, though it was only a little after half past nine. But there was a click, and the gentle, almost childish voice answered.

"Miss Whythe," said Mark quickly. "This is Mark

Saint. We've met a few times; you know, I'm Angelo's father."

There was a little pause. Did the voice become fainter? "Oh. Yes, Mr. Saint."

"I hope I didn't disturb you; I hope you weren't in bed."

"Well, to tell the truth, Mr. Saint—"

Her tone was constrained. Or was it?

His hand clutched the receiver so tightly that his fingers whitened. "Miss Whythe. You live not too far from here. I want to talk with you. I can be there in ten minutes or so, driving fast."

"Tonight?" She sounded a little shrill. "Oh, I'm sorry, Mr. Saint. My granny is in bed; she isn't well. And—I was thinking of going to bed myself, right away. In fact, I have a sedative right here near my hand as I am talking to you now." She paused. "You—you heard about my arm? You are at the party?"

"Yes. May I come, Miss Whythe?"

She was silent so long that he thought she had left him. Then she said, and her voice was frightened—or was it?— "Can't it wait until another time, Mr. Saint?"

"Such as tomorrow? Shall I come to the school?"

Again she was silent. And then he knew. She had not asked him why he wished to see her. She had shown no curiosity at all, no surprise.

"If I have to wait a week, a month, a year, I'll have to see you," he said, almost inaudibly.

Then she faltered, "You make it sound important—I don't know—I'm tired—"

"I know," he said. "I know, my dear. And it is important, extremely important."

"Very well," she said, and hung up abruptly, and he felt the familiar cold sweat on his back again. He ran into the cool night, not stopping to find his coat and hat. He found his car, wedged between others, and savagely he threw the car forward against the bumper ahead, and then back against another bumper, and was finally free. The streets were quiet; he exceeded the speed limit. Within ten minutes or less he was in the quiet fringe of his own suburb, a much poorer fringe, of duplexes crowded together behind the smallest of lawns, with no garages for the little, old cars at the curbs. Jane Whythe lived in a white duplex. A light was shining in the living-room window; he saw the usual white lamp with ruffled pink shade on its table just behind the glass, and a glimpse of the tiniest of living rooms. Jane, herself, opened the door for him, and he saw how pale she was under her mass of riotous brown curls; he saw her right arm in its splints and sling. She looked like a little girl of ten, not a woman of twenty or slightly more. She led him into the living room without speaking, mutely indicated a cheap but brightly chintzed chair, and sat down on a brown mohair sofa across from him. Her pretty features had a withdrawn look, and her colorless mouth was carved and still and her eyes fixed themselves on him like a stricken child awaiting punishment.

He leaned toward her, and tried to smile. "I'm sorry about your accident," he said. She glanced away from him and murmured that he was very kind.

"I heard how it happened," he went on.

Her eyes suddenly flew to his face, and she smiled brilliantly. "Oh, I knew it would be all right! I knew I was wrong. He—" Then she paused, as she saw Mark's face, and her smile vanished.

"No," said Mark, and vaguely wondered how it was possible to feel like this and not have a heart attack. "If you mean Angelo, he didn't tell me, Miss Whythe. I could have lied to you and said he did, and then you would have told me. But I couldn't lie to you, you see."

Her face became shut and still, her eyes very wide. Her left hand, so small and delicate, trembled on her knee. Then she said slowly and carefully, "I don't know what you're talking about, Mr. Saint. I can see, now, that you were told at the party about my arm, and those big, running boys who didn't notice me in front of the rocks— after all, my coat is about the same color and it was a dull day, and I should have been more careful. And I was late; the boys weren't expecting a teacher to jump right up in front of them that way. It—it was all my fault. And now—"

He lifted his hand, as she was about to get up. "Please wait, Miss Whythe. I'm going to be frank with you. This isn't the first time—things—have happened. Don't you understand? It isn't the first time. I can't tell you—I'm Angelo's father, and I love him very much. He's my son; I love him very much. I have to be certain for once. Just once! Try to understand; think if it were your child. Wouldn't you want to know? For his sake?"

For a moment, for just a moment, her young features softened as if she were about to cry in pity and understanding, and then they became resolutely shut again, and her eyes were full of fear. "I still don't know what you mean, Mr. Saint. If you—if you think that perhaps Angelo pushed me, or—fell—into me—perhaps he did. I don't know. If he did, if any boy did, it was unintentional. It happened so very fast; it's still a blur to me. I couldn't believe it when I found myself on the rocks."

"What are you afraid of?" he asked gently. "Angelo? If you are, then all the more reason I should know. If—he did something to you once, he'll do it to you again." And he contemplated what he said with a fresh new horror and his head swam.

Jane was also seeing the horror. As if it were happening now she saw the great boys racing toward her in the dim light, shouting, scuffling, diving, rolling, and she heard her loud and warning shout, and automatically, only sensing rather than actually seeing her, they had swerved aside instinctively. Except for one boy running swiftly and silently on the edge of a group, slightly apart from them, yet with them. She saw his face, immensely enlarged in her sudden knowledge of him and her fright, and then, as she began to lift her slight arm to protect herself she saw his eyes, brilliant as a tiger's eyes, and as appalling, so close to hers, and then his shoulder had struck the rising arm and she was in the air, and then on the stones, breathless and crushed, and she heard and felt the snapping of her arm. None of the boys had seen what had happened, and who had done it, so intent were they on their excited and tumultuous play, and they were far from her before she had the breath and the full consciousness to scream.

Mark was watching her; he saw the dilating and the darkening of her eyes, the way her lower lip was clenched between her teeth.

"It could happen again," he repeated. "To you. To others."

Jane saw the tiger's eyes once more, full upon her even in that gloom, burning with hatred and the lust to destroy, and she shook her head, dazed. She had thought of it often; for a day or two she had been convinced that the boy had realized the advantage of his being with other boys, of being a part of the tussling and roaring mob, and that he had seized that advantage. He had been lying in wait for such an opportunity, and then it was presented to him, and in the swiftness of his splendid mind he had not hesitated. In a way, she had thought, sickened, it had been sheer genius. And then, as the days went by she became less and less convinced that her accident had been intentional. A young boy, almost a little boy, in age if not in strength and height! Children simply did not do such things, unless they were sub-average in intelligence, or like mindless animals! Boys like Angelo Saint were civilized; they came from excellent families; they were loved, protected, and sheltered. They did not come from "broken homes" where savagery was a part of life and hatred a familiar emotion. Jane Whythe was very young, and very innocent. She believed that love was a blessing, that those who possessed it were gentled by it. She had taken a course in child psychology, and had had it beaten into her mind that "bad children" did not exist, only "bad parents," and that it was slum children alone, "the underprivileged one-third of a nation," without advantages and love and cherishing, who were capable of doing deliberate evil, and plotting evil.

She opened her soft mouth to deny, and then seeing Mark's face again, she was silent. What had he said? "It isn't the first time." She studied Mark's face; she thought of the devoted mother; she had once passed the beautiful house and had seen Angelo playing on the lawns. Oh, it wasn't possible! This poor man was neurotic, full of complexes and boundless suspicions.

And then she unaccountably thought of Kennie Richards; she thought of the whole month of March, and then she thought of her struggles with him, her prayers for him, which had come to nothing. She thought of the Miss Knowles, the teacher in Boston, and the Dr. McDowell, who were jointly paying the boy's fees at Miss Simmons' school, and buying his clothing, and visiting him, and giving him the love he had never had before. And her girl's face flamed with wrath.

Poor Kennie, poor little Kennie! He had come to the school, hopeful and bright-eyed and eager. His teachers were proud of him. He had skipped a grade, for Miss Simmons did not believe in children remaining in their "age groups," as there lay disaster for the superior child who was so urgently needed in his country. It was only January when he had reached Jane's class. She knew his history, his whole story. The history of every child was minutely recorded in files locked in Miss Simmons' room, and the teachers alone had access to them in order to know their students fully, so that they would know when to help and when to withhold help, when to be stern and when to be affectionate, and what to expect at all times.

Only Jane and Kennie's other teachers, former teachers in the school, and Miss Simmons had known that Kennie was the son of a drunken murderer, and a murdered mother. She had been exceptionally kind to him, and he had responded gratefully. She could see his gray eyes even now, aglow with intelligence, and his shy and sensitive face. The boys had liked him very much and accepted him. They had known only that he was an orphan; they vaguely believed that wealthy relatives were supporting him. He had never become as popular as the flamboyant Angelo, with his captivating smiles, his rich laughs, his air of assurance, but still he had been much liked.

It was some time before Jane realized that of all the boys only Angelo did not like Kennie. Was it because he suspected that Kennie might be a rival some day? It was impossible to know. Jane only sensed the dislike; she could not actually recall any occasion when Angelo had been offensive to Kennie. She saw with a sort of inner eye; she also saw that these two never had anything to say to each other, that they avoided each other.

One day when alone with Kennie, she had said to him, "I know it's none of my business, Kennie, but has something happened between you and Angelo?"

Why had he colored? But he had said honestly, looking into her eyes, "No, nothing Miss Whythe. It's just that I don't like him and he doesn't like me."

"But Angelo's such a popular boy; everyone likes him!"

Kennie still looked into her eyes. "Do you like him, Miss Whythe?"

"Why, cer—" Then Jane had paused, and blushed herself. She had not thought of it before but suddenly she realized that she was the only teacher, and perhaps the only one in the school, who did not like Angelo Saint. It had not come to her conscious mind before, for she vehemently believed that all children were much superior to adults, that they were a special race apart, to be cherished, to be protected. In fact, she almost if not quite believed that they never grew up, that they remained forever what they were: helpless, dependent, uncorrupted, clean, timelessly innocent. She was always surprised to see little children she had known grow up and become tall, often taller than she. In some way she was hurt by this, even though she knew it was ridiculous. But she always thought of them as The Children, the golden ones, the imperishable, the treasures.

She was very uncomfortable with Kennie for a few moments, for she was embarrassed with herself. But what was it about Angelo Saint that she did not like? She could not explain it, and she was ashamed. Kennie was smiling at her, a kind, adult smile, and he had actually patted her hand which was smaller than his own and said, "Never mind. It isn't important, Miss Whythe. Maybe you wouldn't understand. It's just that I've caught on about Angelo, and he knows it."

"What have you caught on?"

Kennie hesitated, and then shuffled his feet. "Oh, I don't know. I just think that he's a fake. Kind of like an actor, or something. You know not real. Just pretending."

"Why, for goodness sake? Why should he?"

"I don't know, Miss Whythe. And maybe I'm wrong."

She had looked closely at Angelo the next day, and all at once he had glanced up and met her eyes, and though he instantly smiled his charming smile his eyes became cold and watchful and full of thought. She had been uneasy with him after that, and he knew it, and she was angry at herself and a little angry with Kennie. After all, only children who had been browbeaten, ignored, "rejected," and unwanted, learned to be deceitful for their own protection. That is what they had taught her in her child-psychology classes during her education courses, and then in adolescent psychology. But had there not been a hasty and almost unwilling exploration into the child-psychopath mind, too? It was as if her prof had been annoyed by that brief excursion, and had not believed it, and had not wanted to believe that some children are innately evil and not the "victims" of "problem" parents, inferior environment and what he obscurely called "local discriminations and social restrictions and inequities." She had thought then, though a young girl: Why is there such an insistence these days on believing that all wrong and all wickedness and crime do not exist of themselves, but are the results of what is vaguely called "conditions?"

If anyone, she thought as she looked at Kennie's generous face and firm, honest lips and intelligent eyes, had a right to be maladjusted, evil, twisted in nature, asocial, delinquent, cruel and uncontrollable, then Kennie was the one. But he was not. He was the living refutation of theory; he had been unloved and rejected, beaten and despised, brutally treated by both parents from almost his very birth. Yet he was gentle and strong, kind and loving, full of sympathy and understanding, responsive at once to friendship and completely responsible. It was very disconcerting.

All had gone well until a certain day. She had asked Kennie to stand up and read from the current book the class was studying, for he had an excellent and resonant voice. But as he stood up a page fell from his book, and from the little distance at which she sat Jane saw that it was scrawled over with characters written in red pencil. A neighboring boy had politely reached down and picked it up for Kennie, but his eyes had been caught by the writing, and he had looked aghast. Suddenly curious, other boys leaned from their desks and read. They said nothing. The first boy handed it to Kennie, who read it. He had suddenly paled, looked mortally sick, and fallen into his seat, speechlessly.

Jane had come at once from her seat and taken the sheet of paper. She read, as from a kind of dossier: "Kenneth Landowski (alias Richards). Son of Stanislaus Landowski and Eva Landowski, deceased. Born January

3, 1953 in the City. Stanislaus Landowski, a laborer and drunkard, and chronically unemployed, had been on welfare with his family from April 2, 1956 to June 19, 1958, and had received psychiatric treatment from Drs. ——— and ———, with no result of an encouraging nature. On June 5, 1959, he had murdered his wife Eva, and had been executed in Sing Sing on January 4, 1959. Only witness, son Kenneth, who had to be sent to a children's nursing home for a period of one year, mind affected." Then, in large block printing was the query: "Do we want a person of this background among us?"

Jane had thought she would faint. She heard a dim sibilant sound, and looked about her. The news was traveling from boy to boy, moving swiftly like a serpent from desk to desk. Kennie sat as if struck dead, his eyes staring emptily before him. Jane had then touched his shoulder, bent to smile into his face, then had taken the paper to her desk. She had held it up to the class, and all the boys watched her intently.

"You've heard about anonymous letters, written by cruel and malicious people," she said. "This is a sample. It was meant to hurt Kennie, whom we all like and respect. Why, I don't know. There is a wicked boy in this class. I won't ask him to show himself; he won't. But, as certainly as he has an immortal soul, both God and man will punish him, finally, for this unprovoked attack on Kennie. And this is what we do with anonymous letters, and if you boys ever receive them in the future, do the same." She had opened her bag and taken out her lighter and burned the letter, and the boys had watched the flame like children hypnotized. She had then resumed the class.

But from that day on Kennie was avoided, uncomfortably. And he withdrew, with pride. It was never the same. Finally a mother or two appeared indignantly in Miss Simmons' office, and had been dismissed, tartly. The question remained, however, how this information from Kennie's dossier had been made available to some boy in the class. The file which contained the boys' histories was always locked, and only Miss Simmons had the key. Jane had given it great thought. If a teacher wished to refresh her memory about a boy she had only to ask Miss

Simmons for the key, and it was given her in Miss Simmons' presence, and then returned at once. Of course, Miss Simmons herself frequently opened the file. It was a terrible mystery. Then Kennie, only a month ago, had come to both Jane and Miss Simmons and had quietly asked to be released from the school. He said he thought he would prefer public school. Arguments did nothing; the boy had a determined nature. He left.

Miss Simmons had asked every boy in the class, separately, if he had ever found her key and opened the file. Each one vehemently denied it, and with indignation. He had been believed. Jane did not mention it, but she remembered that Miss Simmons was an old lady and sometimes absently left the key in the lock, herself, until some teacher rescued and returned it. Jane herself had come upon the file once or twice with the key fixed in the lock. Some boy—but who?—had seized the opportunity to peer with animal curiosity at the history of his friends, or to see what had been written about himself. But why had Kennie been singled out? The teachers had been questioned; they had been in and out of Miss Simmons' office frequently, a few days before the scarring note had been found. They could not recall any single boy as being present during their visits, though sometimes Miss Simmons was absent at the time.

Now Jane, thinking about Kennie, looked at Mark Saint. Her eyes were abstracted, and she repeated what she had said: "I don't know. Mr. Saint. I can't make accusations on anything so nebulous."

"Yes," said Mark, in a sick voice, "everything is always so nebulous. And so clever."

"Perhaps you are doing Angelo an injustice," said Jane, the child psychologist, the child lover, the child defender. Mark gave her a cigarette, and they smoked together in a little silence. Jane was becoming more confident, and she regarded Mark with severity. Was he, after all, a really "understanding" parent? He loved Angelo, but perhaps did not devote as much time to the boy as he should. Otherwise, how could he think such things of him? A man should spend at least two hours with his son every day, and every weekend. That is what she had been taught. Of course, the fact that a man might have business on those weekends, or work to do at night, or friends to cultivate, was of no importance when it concerned The Children. The Children were all.

Jane did not know at what instant, while she was sitting there tranquilly smoking and rebuking Mark in her stern young mind, that a picture, clear and vivid, rose up in her mind, and shocked her so much that she dropped her cigarette. Mark bent and picked it up, and saw the shock on her face, and he said softly, "Well, what is it, my dear?"

But Jane did not hear him. She was remembering a certain day when she had gone into Miss Simmons' office for something which she could not now recall. Angelo Saint had been sitting in the visitor's chair, waiting, with an envelope in his hand. It was lunchtime, and she had pleasantly asked him why he was not in the cafeteria. "Oh, I've already had my lunch, Miss Whythe," he had answered in his rich and cajoling voice, and he had stood up at once with his perfect manners. "I have an invitation here, for dinner, for Miss Simmons, from my mother. I could have laid it on her desk, but I thought it would be more polite to give it to her in person." His thick dark brows had knitted anxiously, and he had looked at her with a winning question in his eyes. "Don't you think that is the best way?"

"Of course," she said at once, trying to smother her instinctive dislike for him which she would not acknowledge even to herself. It was just that uneasiness. . . . "But don't stay here after the bell rings if Miss Simmons hasn't returned, will you?"

She had not looked at the file to see if Miss Simmons had again forgotten to take the key out. Why should she have? She was not concerned with the file that day; she could not recall, now, just what her errand had been. But she had left Angelo, smiling, in his chair, waiting for Miss Simmons.

She had no proof! she thought passionately to herself, avoiding Mark's eyes. No proof at all. If the key had been there, if Angelo had seen it, if he had taken the opportunity to open the file and read, if no teacher had entered, if he had done it swiftly, if he had had this in mind for a long time . . . So many ifs, and all of them vague and not to be proved, and each depending on the other, in an incredible chain of events.

"Help me," said Mark. "If there is just one thing that troubles you, one thing you can be sure of, one thing that will help Angelo."

"You're not sure yourself about anything," said Jane, and though she was still seeing that picture of Angelo in the office, she shook her head. "Brilliant children often do things that adults misunderstand. It can always be easily explained—if a parent takes the time, and has the love and patience and understanding to find out." Her dark eyes admonished him, accused him. He stood up, and looked down at her a long time. Then he spoke almost inaudibly:

"Little Jane Whythe. You know something, you suspect something, and you won't tell me, out of a misguided sense of justice. My dear child, listen to me. You're still in danger, if Angelo did that to you deliberately. Or perhaps he's satisfied now. I hope so! But someday, he won't be satisfied—oh, my God!—with just hurting someone! Someday, if he isn't stopped now, and perhaps treated, he will—"

Jane frowned at him formidably. What awful things to say about "a child," and especially on the part of "a parent"! Why, the poor man needed psychiatric treatment immediately, and "tender, loving care"! She blurted out, "Mr. Saint, you look very tired and worn. In that condition," she continued primly, "one needs help."

"Angelo needs help," said Mark, in a fading voice.

"He does, indeed," said Jane, and stood up with tiny dignity, dismissing him. "He needs his father's love and interest." She was certain now, after talking with Mark, that the things she had vaguely feared and suspected were only shadows, and she was filled with contrition and determination to give more time to Angelo and understand him. And she was ashamed. For the first time she loved Angelo, in her pity for him that he had such a father—neurotic, almost hysterical, high-strung, and apparently consumed with dislike for his son. Was there an Oedipus complex in the background? Were father and son competing for the affection of the wife and mother? Oh, that explained everything! Jane gave Mark a knowing smile, and shook hands with him.

CHAPTER ELEVEN

"You aren't eating your dinner, dear," said Kathy to her husband. "And I fried that chicken myself. Betty doesn't do it right. And I made the hollandaise sauce; I don't like the prepared variety. It's your favorite dinner, and you aren't eating a thing! I'm hurt."

"Sorry, darling," said Mark, and put his fork into a succulent chicken leg. But the utensil was heavy in his fingers; his stomach turned. Kathy was regarding him anxiously. "I do wish you'd go to Dr. Hauser, and not Dr. Bowes. You haven't had your yearly check-up. Mark, you must have lost at least ten pounds, and you can't afford it!"

"I've been working hard," said Mark. "Please don't worry. We have a new contract, and it's tricky." Angelo ate with his usual finicky care, but he watched his father through his eyelashes. So, the old boy was still thinking of that stinker, dear Auntie Alicia! Much good it would do him. He, Angelo, had effectively scared her away, forever. Now, there was no threat to his good and happy life, and no unexpected visits when he had to see her ugly watching face. Above all, her nasty watching face, which could never be deceived. There were few people in Angelo's world now who dared to threaten him by understanding him or withholding adulation from him. Even that stupid Jane Whythe had at last succumbed; she couldn't do enough for him. She murmured at him affectionately; she had him read his compositions in class, and led the applause. She had told him, over and over, with intent, sedulous emphasis, that some day he would be a great artist of some kind, which affirmed his own opinion. He had been on guard for a time, watching for any sign that she had known all about that broken-arm episode. He

131

had seen it for at least ten school days, and had plotted again. But then, all at once, the suspicion was gone, and had been replaced by affection, admiration and sincere acceptance. Angelo had an idea what had happened: She had brooded on the matter for a couple of weeks, and then had settled it in her own mind as unjust and unpardonable on her part. She was compensating now for her earlier coldness and suspicion, and he wallowed in it with malicious pleasure and enjoyment. She was safe; he no longer had to waste time thinking of something more drastic. In a way that was disappointing; he so enjoyed those episodes of secret violence. But a fellow couldn't have everything, he thought philosophically. Everything was fine. Kennie Richards, or Landowski, had vanished, like the others he hated, from his life.

Sometimes even Angelo paused to wonder if he loved his parents. Of course, Mum was an idiot, but she adored him. He supposed he loved her; he would love her more if she would just stop wearing those foolish whirling skirts and pretending to be young for his sake. At any rate, she was indispensable. He could not imagine a world empty of her idolatry, empty of her admiration and the gifts and comforts and luxuries she heaped on him. He was the very center of her world, as he was the center of his. Nothing could menace the place he had in her life; nothing could remove him from the core of her existence. When he had been younger, he had been enraged when his parents had embraced in his presence. But that was before he realized that Mark was nothing to Kathy compared with her son. Let him have the crumbs! He was a crumb himself.

He did not actively dislike his father; there were even times when he was fond of Mark, especially when Mark unexpectedly brought home a lavish gift. But was he the center of Mark's life? At five, the doubt had inflamed the boy with fury. But now that he was ten he understood that if his life were to be surrounded with pleasant things and all that he wished, Mark must have another life besides his son, a life concerned with business which brought in a great deal of money. So Angelo indulgently forgave his father for not centering every thought and every deed upon him. This did not prevent him from annoying Mark at times; after all, a fellow had a right to a little fun. And the best joy of all was making game of Mum in Mark's presence. It was really funny to see the vexation in Mark's eyes, and how he had to restrain himself from speaking. Oh, people were imbeciles! They were expressly created for the exploitation and use and pleasure of the Angelos of the world, and in particular Angelo Saint. Angelo enjoyed his life very much. But he was always on guard to see that no one else menaced that paradise by dislike, by understanding him, by demanding their own rights in preference to his own desires. Even Mark's infrequent punishments, such as a stern rebuke or sending him away from the table, and even the one and only occasion when he had physically punished his son, had been forgiven. They assured Angelo that his father was also engrossed with him even if he had other interests in the world outside.

Preternaturally acute though he was, and always watchful, Angelo did not know that while Mark was listlessly playing with his food he was not thinking of Alice Knowles. Angelo did not know that Mark was thinking of him, for Mark had never indicated to the boy that he had his fearful suspicions and secret terrors about him. Not once did the boy suspect this, for was he not the most clever creature in the world, and were not his parents stupid and incapable of mistrust or dark conjecture with regard to their son? As for all the others, they too had been stupid. But that was because he was so superior to them in every way, and so adroit, and never left any untidy ends floating about. Sometimes he told himself, virtuously, that it was not his fault at all. The others were the culprits.

Mark said, the food in his mouth nauseating him, "When are we going to have Jack McDowell and that nice girl of his to dinner? We were at the engagement party and other parties in their honor."

"Oh, I'm going to give Mary a shower soon," said Kathy restlessly. "Frankly, though, I don't care much for either of them. Mary puts on airs, just because her father was a famous surgeon in the City, and Jack has a way of—peering. It's an occupational disease of psychiatrists, I suppose."

Angelo was alerted. He hated Dr. McDowell with an intense hatred. Jack had always been most kind to him, and had listened seriously when Angelo had spoken. But he listened! He had a listening air, as if hearing beyond mere words, and he especially had that air when he was present in this house. A subtle threat hung about him, for all his consideration, for all his pleasant words, and the threat was to Angelo. There was nothing Angelo could do about it, for the doctor was beyond his reach, but Angelo had had the most satisfying daydreams of how he would eliminate one whom he considered his enemy. No one must listen to what Angelo Saint really thought!

Kathy sighed patiently. "All right, how about a week from tonight? I'll call Mary, and you call Jack. I suppose it's only the courteous thing to do."

HE would be here again, the threat, the listener! Angelo put down his fork and glared at his mother, and the skin about his mouth whitened. Of course, he could be away that night, at the home of one of his devoted friends. But Angelo made it a point to be present when the doctor was here. A person couldn't tell what he might say to his parents in his absence, dangerous things. Dr. McDowell "understood." On his last visit he had hardly taken his eyes from the boy, and there had been a most curious expression in them.

"No!" shouted Angelo, and struck the tablecloth with his fork.

Kathy was amazed. "I thought you liked Jack," she said. "He's always so nice to you, and treats you like an adult, unlike some others I could name," she added with annoyance.

Mark asked quietly, "Why not, son?"

Angelo's nostrils distended. Careful, he told himself. They mustn't suspect why he hated Jack McDowell. That would make them curious; they might ask the doctor questions which would disrupt his world and ruin it.

"I don't like him," said Angelo, meticulously picking his words and looking at his parents meltingly. "Oh, I'm ashamed to tell you why." He peeped at Kathy as if begging her forgiveness in advance.

"Oh, do tell us, darling!" she sang.

So Angelo folded his hands on the table and took on a serious, manly expression and let his big light brown eyes fix themselves sincerely on his mother. "It's just that I have a feeling he let Aunt Alicia down, and that's why she went away. I think she expected him to marry her, and then when she found out he'd just been taking up her time and had no intention of marrying her, she couldn't stand it. After all, she's my aunt, part of the family and so I resent him."

"Do you hear that, Mark!" cried Kathy in rapture, striking her hands together and clasping her fingers and glowing like a light "Oh, the darling, the darling! How he bleeds for others! He's so sensitive, so wonderful! So—feeling!"

Mark said nothing. Angelo did not see the sudden fixity on his father's face, the sudden resolution, the sudden thought. Kathy sprang up girlishly from her chair and rushed to her son and embraced and kissed him in a flurry of ecstatic passion.

"But you're wrong, darling, darling!" bubbled Kathy. "How unjust, and that isn't like you at all! Jack did want to marry Alicia; she told us that herself."

"I don't believe it," said Angelo soberly. "I think she was just saving her pride."

"It could be, oh, it could be!" cried Kathy, with compassion. " 'Out of the mouths of babes and sucklings!' " She sat down and regarded her son as if he were a miracle.

"Nonsense," said Mark bitterly. "Angelo's only using his imagination. And it was Jack, remember, Kathy, who told us he wanted to marry Alice and she refused."

"I don't believe it!" said Kathy emphatically, still staring fascinated at her son. "Children are very subtle. Angelo struck right at the heart of it all! Under the circumstances, considering how he treated Alicia, I just can't be friendly to Jack. And all the time the real truth was right under our noses!" she added, marveling. "He just wanted to ingratiate himself with us, and that is why he lied."

"Why should he want to ingratiate himself with us?" asked Mark. "He has hundreds of friends. He's very respected, and is called in on many consultations by other psychiatrists. He isn't the affected kind, with an accent and owlish glasses. And he's independently wealthy too, and is socially accepted in circles where even we can't penetrate. What benefit could we give him?"

"Oh, psychiatrists are always looking for patients," said

Kathy, dismissing her husband's remarks. She leaned toward Angelo, and touched his hand as one would touch a saint. "Even a rich doctor isn't going to overlook an opportunity for twenty dollars to fifty dollars an hour."

"So, we aren't going to invite them, then?"

"No, not *en famille*. I'll talk to some of the girls. We can make it a big restaurant party. I won't have him here, hurting Angel."

Mark looked at his son, and his gray lips tightened. So, he thought, you've won again, and I think I know what was in your mind. God help me, and God help you, too, my son.

Mark became aware, for the first time, of the soft hum of the air-conditioner on this warm late afternoon in June. He became aware that he had been talking steadily, with anguish, occasionally with panic and frenzy, for a long time, though he had tried to keep his voice reasonable and quiet. And he had not been interrupted once.

Dr. McDowell had listened, his light blue eyes fixed earnestly on the tormented other man, his hands clasped together on the leather top of his fine desk. He had not moved, except to light an occasional cigarette. He had asked no questions. He had only listened.

It was cool in the large and airy office, with its friendly furniture, its reassuringly handsome draperies, its excellent rug. Yet Mark repeatedly wiped his ashen face with his handkerchief, until the linen was a sodden lump in his hand.

"There it is; all of it," said Mark finally, and in a hoarse voice. "Tell me I'm insane. Tell me I'm a neurotic. Tell me I'm out of my mind, and need psychiatric treatment."

"In short," said the doctor gently, "tell you anything but the truth."

Mark's heart jumped savagely, then beat with a sickening rhythm.

"What do you mean, Jack?" he asked. "The truth?"

The doctor stood up, thrust his hands into his pockets and walked slowly around the room, his head bent. Then he stopped before Mark and contemplated him somberly. "You're his father," he said. "Parents don't want to be told. . . . They'll do anything to avoid that. They want to be reassured; they even want to be told they're crazy themselves, and should be confined. They'd find that easier to bear. For they love their children."

Mark looked dazedly at the lump of soiled cloth in his hands. He felt as though he were dying.

"Then you believe me?" he whispered. "You don't think I'm imagining things, inventing things, that I've been having hallucinations?"

Jack sat down again, and now he looked at his clasped hands. He waited a moment or two, then he opened a drawer and took out a bottle of good whiskey and two glasses. "Let's have a drink," he said. "No, don't wave it away. There are a lot of times when a drink is a lifesaver. And this is one of them. Frankly, I don't like your color. You've been living under a terrible strain for a long time. I'll give you the name of a good cardiologist. I don't think, however, that it is organic; I think it's functional in your case." And no wonder, he added to himself in commiseration.

Mark forced himself to drink. All at once he did not want to know the truth. He had come here to be laughed at in a friendly fashion; he had come here to have his fears blown away. He had even come to be told that he was mad. Anything. He finished the drink; he stared down into the empty glass with eyes that had no expression. A dark lock of his hair slipped on his wet forehead.

"I shouldn't have come," he said dully.

"Of course you should have," said Jack. "If only for your own sake. Mark, I'm going to tell you the truth. Your son is a psychopath, and there is no cure for him, though other doctors are experimenting with shock treatments and everything else. Your son is an atavist, a throwback. In his own way he is as normal as anyone else; he's as normal as any boy born in a cave tens of thousands of years ago. He isn't insane, if that is what you fear. He could pass examinations brilliantly. In fact, he's eminently sane. It's just that he's been born with a lack, just as some children are born physically lacking an arm or a leg, sight or hearing. And that lack is what we call conscience. There are some Freudians, even today, who insist that conscience is an acquired trait, forced on

children by parents and theologians, and that no child is
born with it. I disagree. There was an experiment made
... but that isn't relevant to Angelo at this time. Man
is born a moral creature; he can be perverted, later,
but he was born moral, and with a conscience. That has
been proved over and over, until there isn't the slightest
doubt left. I interviewed some Nazis long after the war,
who had been brought up to have no conscience, who
were allowed no religious teachings, who were taught
almost from babyhood to be ruthless and cruel and even
murderous when commanded. They knew nothing else but
violence and hatred. And yet, while I was talking with
them many of them burst into tears and told me how they
had loathed what they were, even as children, and hated
themselves as men, and had covertly assisted potential
victims of the Gestapo. Some of their friends, caught in
this very thing, had either committed suicide, or had been
executed. But they had taken this risk.

"Why? Because almost all men are born with a moral
conscience, and nothing can extirpate it, not even a Hitler,
not even a Stalin, not even a Khrushchev. Why do you
suppose that hundreds of Soviet soldiers refused to fire on
the Hungarian revolutionaries, and permitted themselves to
be shot rather than to murder little children and wom-
en and men who loved their country and loved their
God? Some are weak enough to try to smother their
conscience and their human compassion, and conceal them
in self-defense. But others prefer to die rather than live
with themselves and their memories. And those Communist boys, so many of them, chose death to the final
violation of their natures. The heroes aren't the killers;
they are often the killed, perhaps they are the only heroes.
And I might remind you that those Communist boys had
never been taught anything about God or conscience or
morality, or right or wrong except how it advanced the
cause of Sovietism. You see, God is never absent from the
hearts of men."

"But, He is absent from Angelo's."

"Yes. You see, nature has a way of destroying the atavists in the womb, or building in a mechanism which will
destroy them in early childhood. But prenatal care of mothers, and antibiotics and scientific feeding of infants, have

kept these atavists alive, and flourishing. Too, some Evil, and the Church calls it Lucifer, often gives these atavists a superior constitution so that they can survive, and superior intelligence, so that they can destroy. The atavists are spiritually retarded, if you want to put it that way."

He paused and looked at the distracted father. "You aren't a Catholic. If I talk to you of inborn evil, you may smile indulgently. After all, don't the child psychologists say every child is born perfect, but is corrupted by parents later? Of course, that is false. Satan is unusually vital and dominant in the world now. The time is imminent when we, who have consciences, must face those who have no consciences—the atavists. It is a terrible fact that these atavists now control the world."

Mark was thinking of his beautiful and vital son. "Angelo is the favorite of our minister. He sings in the choir. He is at the head of his Sunday-school class. He reads the Bible, and can discuss it intelligently with us. He is in the Boy Scouts. He belongs to local boys' groups. . . ."

"Yes. Of course. He has learned what is socially acceptable, what is socially desired, what is expected. And he always wants to please—for his own awful ends. And, in his heart, as a realistic atavist, he laughs at us. He is one with the saber-toothed tiger, the dinosaur, the tyrannosaurus. He is, spiritually, the inhabitant of the mighty fern-filled jungle, the steaming pits. He belongs with the birth of the world; he knows the ancient convulsions, the hot, pouring rains, the volcanoes. Is it his fault? No. Nature is in flux; sometimes the old patterns intrude; they haven't been bred out yet."

Jack fumbled with a cigarette. "Do you think, for one instant, that Angelo is moved by the prayers in your church, that he believes, for one moment, the glorious story of the Incarnation and the Crucifixion? Of course not! To him, they are childish fairy stories. But they are accepted. Therefore, to be accepted he must accept them also, at least outwardly. They do not touch his heart; but he sees that they touch other hearts. He doesn't want to be an outcast, a pariah. So he pretends to be touched, too. Don't blame him! He is what he is, and no one can change him."

"Jack, is it something in our ancestry, Kathy's or mine? Are we at fault, in some way?"

"Of course not! An imbecile, an idiot, a retarded child, a feeble-minded child, an atavist like Angelo, can be born in any family. They are primitives, hangovers from the race's infant years. Before God touched humanity with His light-filled finger and called forth a soul in man."

"You are trying to tell me that Angelo was born without a soul?"

Jack was silent a moment. And then he said, "Yes. Perhaps. His soul is embryonic. It may be there, but it isn't developed. It has been—delayed. I don't know, Mark, and no other psychiatrist knows either, though some pretend to, out of pity for parents."

"And nothing can develop Angelo's soul?"

"Nothing. He hasn't one, or it is still embryonic. Malformed; not developed."

"What do we do with him?" And Mark thought of his wife, and winced.

"At the best, you can help him with his pretendings, not for his sake, but for the sake of others. You can help him take on coloration, and convince him that unless he does he will perish in some way. And these people are always so protective of themselves. You can appeal to their greatly intelligent selves, and nothing else."

"Angelo—he's so charming. Everyone loves him."

"Naturally. That is the atavist's disguise. And don't think they don't work hard to acquire that disguise! They work like hell. Only their families get a glimpse of their saber-toothed selves, occasionally. I treat so-called neurotics everyday who are married to atavists. I can't advise a divorce, being a Catholic, but I do advise separation before a tragedy happens."

Mark could not speak. He thought of his beautiful son, his clever and intelligent son. And he knew now that his son was part of a mist-filled age millennia in the past, and no part of this age. No wonder he found the spiritually developed ridiculous, for his world in himself was ruled by tooth and claw, red and dripping, hungry and devouring.

Jack said, "There is something else I must tell you. Angelo tried to kill Alice some years ago. She told me." He held his breath and waited for Mark to cry out.

But Mark only listened and nodded repeatedly, automatically. Of course, he had always really known that. He listened to Jack's story of what had happened to the innocent little dog, and still he nodded. He was so ill that, to stop the endless nodding, he had to put his hands forcibly on his head. "I have been hiding," he said at last, in a strange voice. "Jack, why can't we have a law to do away with them?"

"We are humanitarians," said Jack wryly. "We think all creatures born in the shape of man are men. Now, come. Would you consent, right now, to having Angelo mercifully and painlessly killed, as you would in the case of any other incomplete animal?"

Mark did not answer. Jack said, "What is evil? Is it atavism? Is it Satanism? I don't know! But it is both of these, I think."

Mark put his arm on the desk, for he was exhausted, and he bent his head to it. "What do we do now?"

"I've told you. Don't be so discouraged. Psychopaths, or atavists, sometimes, quite often, make what we lightheartedly call an adjustment. That is, they learn to conform for their own gain and profit. Angelo may grow up to be a most magnetic and successful man. I can tell you this, he'll never be a neurotic! To be a neurotic, you have to have a soul, to be earnestly and terribly soul-aware and suffering. Angelo, if protected, if constantly assured of his superiority, may make you proud some day. But I pity his wife and children."

Mark felt as if he weighed several tons. His flesh dragged on his bones. He looked at the palms of his hands. "I'm worried. That is putting it mildly. Kathy is over forty. She's pregnant. She learned that a couple of weeks ago. Now, must we worry about having another— psychopath, an atavist?"

Jack got up and came to him swiftly. "Does Angelo know?"

Mark looked at him, dazed. "No. Kathy thinks he is still a baby. And she's embarrassed about conceiving at her age. But I've thought, perhaps a brother or a sister might help Angelo. . . ."

Jack was greatly concerned. He rolled a cigarette over and over in his fingers. "When will the baby be born?"

"October."

"Maybe he shouldn't be told for a while."

"Why? He's going on eleven. He's been taught all about sex; Kathy made a point of that. She's eagerly answered all his questions ever since he was five years old. And he probably now knows more about sex than Kathy does."

Jack looked at the cigarette in his fingers. "How is Kathy taking this?"

"I told you—embarrassed. But lately, she is becoming 'radiant' again. She is bursting to tell Angelo, but controls herself. She doesn't want to worry him, she says. He may be concerned that his mother might not survive. That is what she says."

"Would you consider sending him away until the baby is born?" Jack was very pale.

"I thought of that. Camp in July. Boarding school in September. But he doesn't even want to go to camp this summer, though he liked it last year. When I mentioned a fine boarding school—a military school—he screamed like a girl. He was hysterical for days."

He feels something, thought Jack, terribly alarmed. He feels something threatening him, though he doesn't yet know what it is. His sacred, his self-encompassing world—it's in danger, and he doesn't yet know why.

Then Jack mutely lifted his hand. There was nothing he could do.

He said, "I think Angelo should be told at once, by his mother. I think he should be reassured, vehemently, that the coming baby will not threaten his position, that he will be the more important because of it. Do you understand, Mark?"

The two men looked into each other's eyes.

"Does he suspect what you're thinking about him, Mark?"

"I don't know. I've never known what he thought, Jack. But he watches me. When I can't read any longer, and begin to think, there his, right beside me, watching me—as if listening to my thoughts. Jack, is this inherited? Is it possible we can have—another?"

"It isn't inherited. The chance of having another atavist,

or psychopath, is about the same as anyone else's, no more, no less."

"I wish," said Mark, with deadly quiet, "that he had died when he was born."

"Yes. I understand that. And you're not the only parent in the world, in this city, in your own suburbs, perhaps on your own street, who thinks that, too, though he never says it. He hopes against hope."

"Why have we been afflicted this way?"

Why don't you ask God? thought Jack. But he said, "The parents of those born lacking always ask that. It's a mystery."

"Kathy always spoils him. She sings over him, chirps, bubbles, radiates over him. Perhaps——"

"No, Mark. I don't think he would have been better."

Mark stood up and went to the window and looked far down at the busy street, boiling with taxis and buses and automobiles and crowds. It would be so easy! Jack was beside him, his hand on his arm, his face full of compassion. Mark said, staring down blindly, "Jack, do you think he has—killed—anyone yet?"

"Probably not! I told you, they're careful. I don't think he ever intended openly to kill anyone, except Alice. As they grow older, these atavists, they understand they must protect themselves. When Angelo is fourteen he will not only be in the highest fifth of his class, but he will have learned to control himself so well that even you will relax and think it all over."

"It won't be over."

"No. But you may never see any more signs of it. Try to think of the other child. You, too, have a life to live. Forget Angelo, if you can."

"He is my son. I love him."

CHAPTER TWELVE

It was an unusually hot summer. Even the suburbs were hot, and even the country cabin and its surroundings. It was late July. Kathy's voluminous and tilting skirts hid her condition; she had not as yet taken to the blatant floating tunics of other women. "They advertise!" she would say. "Why, *anyone* can have a baby! They put on these silly tunics the first week, then stick out their stomachs. When I was a girl women had a little modesty. They didn't proclaim loudly to the world, in sequined or flaring tunics, that they'd been sleeping lustfully with their husbands and the result was practically in a playpen. Thank goodness Angel doesn't have the slightest suspicion! He would be so embarrassed! Do you know, Mark dear, it came to me as something quite horrifying and shameful, when I was about Angel's age, that my parents had been sleeping together!"

Mark said, smiling, "I know. All kids go through that stage. They like to think, even when they know better, that their own existence happened without natural intervention first. Their parents are 'different' from other parents. They wouldn't do that!"

Kathy sighed; she felt very close to Mark these days. They sat on the porch of the cabin, side by side, hands clasped affectionately together. Angelo was far away, playing with the now devoted Sally and Bobbie. Kathy leaned her head on her husband's shoulder, and he felt a rush of tenderness for her. The obstetrician, who did not approve of middle-aged women having children, especially when there was such a gap between ages as there would be between Angelo and the coming child, had assured Mark that Kathy was in excellent condition and he had nothing to fear. "A little difficult, perhaps, because middle-aged

144

bones aren't as pliable as young bones, but nothing to worry about."

Kathy looked well; her skin had taken on a bloom, her eyes a luster that was not strained and forced. "I suppose I'll have to tell Angel soon," she said. "Perhaps in another month or so, when it just can't be hidden any longer, and I graduate to tunics myself. But I certainly won't wear those coy slacks under them, which make a pregnant woman look like a cantaloupe on sticks."

"Do you want me to tell him, Katherine?"

She meditated, then gave him a sidelong, jealous look. "No. I don't think so. I can make it so sweet; men are so coarse."

"You'll tell him about the birds and the bees, perhaps."

"Mark, don't be so sarcastic! Angel has had a thorough sex education. We've had many talks about it in the past. I've given him an almost—holy—regard for the processes of life—a reverence."

Mark stood up abruptly and went to the porch rail, and he looked at the railing on which Alice had sat, and from which she had been pushed almost to her death.

"I've talked to him, too," said Mark, still looking at the railing. And he thought of the maid, Bertie, and Jane Whythe. Who else had there been, never to be known by him, Mark? Had anyone died?

"Mark," said Kathy suddenly. "You are getting thinner and thinner! You worry me to death, and your color is awful! Oh, I'm afraid! Why don't you go to the doctor?"

"I did," said Mark, not turning. "I even went to a cardiologist. Now, don't get excited. There's nothing wrong. I'm not so young myself any longer, you know. I'm thirty-eight. And, I've been working very hard this year." He paused. "Have you ever thought that Angelo may be jealous, when you tell him? After all, he's been the center of your life ever since he was born. He might not want to share that center with anyone else; he might resent it; a lot of children do, you know."

"Oh, Mark, you never did understand Angel! There isn't a jealous bone in his body! I never heard a word of envy from him! Why, he'll be out of his mind with joy and anticipation. A brother, or a sister, all his own, to cherish, to teach to walk, to love, to watch over!"

Mark thought of the unborn child with a prayer in his heart. A boy? A girl? He hoped for a girl, a kind little creature who would wear long braids with ribbons on the ends, and with stiff little skirts showing pretty underpants. A girl—a companion. Men loved their daughters dearly. They would walk along the street together, hand in hand; she would ride on his shoulder. She would make him forget all his agonies, his longing for Alice, his terror for his son, his impatience with his wife, the looming threat in all the world. When he looked in his daughter's eyes he would forget Angelo. He would protect her from all the Angelos in the world. No young man, in the coming years, would ever be able to deceive him.

"You don't mind now, do you dear?" he asked his wife.

"Oh, no, I'm so happy! I just can't wait to share my happiness with Angel. And isn't it wonderful that we still have Betty, who adores Angel? She is the only one he ever liked."

Thank God for that, thought Mark.

Mark returned to the City after the usual four weeks; he would come back to the cabin only for weekends after this. The house was hot and still and closed. He opened windows and doors. A woman came in every week to dust and clean, so there was no musty smell in the house. But the sun and air lay in hot dead brightness in every room. The silence seemed to ring. Mark took a shower. It was late Sunday afternoon. He went into the garden, neat and colorful with flowers. But he did not want to stay here; everything reminded him of Angelo, and the horror that was Angelo, the saber-toothed tiger that was his son. He thought of calling friends, but he was too tired to talk with them. A walk in the Park, perhaps? It was a long ride into the blazing City, but the Park was cool and dusky, surrounded though it was by the cloudy and pearl-colored towers of apartment buildings and hotels. If he hurried, he could be there long before sunset; he could walk alone along the quiet paths and under the quiet, heavy trees and see no one he knew. The City would be ringing with quiet; everyone who could went to the "country" on the weekends, and those who could not stayed in their sweltering or air-conditioned apartments and later pretended they had spent the two days with unnamed friends near the Sound, or up in Connecticut. Only tourists would be on the streets, and it would be good to see their fresh and wondering faces, their innocent admiring faces.

So Mark drove quickly into the City, parked his car on an almost empty street and walked into the Park. He had not been born in the City; he had not lived here until he was twenty-one. But it had a charm for him beyond the charm of neat suburbs and spacious quiet houses.

Few people were in the Park, though he heard children at a distance laughing at the ponds where they sailed boats, and the barking of pet dogs on leashes. Mark sat on a bench and a cool wind blew against his weary face and ruffled his hair, in which there were new streaks of gray. He smiled as young shy couples passed him, hand in hand. A policeman stopped to exchange talk of the weather and wipe his hot red face. Squirrels ran about on the grass and the birds swore at them, and they returned the oaths in good measure. There was a scent of pine abroad, and leaves glittered on the topmost branches in the lowering sun. The cloudy towers surrounding the Park became incandescent.

A young bareheaded woman and a tall young boy approached Mark's bench. They were laughing happily at each other; the boy's laugh was full and strong, and did not sound like Angelo's—rich and warming and full of beguilement. Mark turned his head and looked full into Alice's face.

She stopped instantly, as if shocked, and, as he slowly rose, she turned scarlet. But she was all composure. She shook hands with him gravely, and smiled her beautiful smile, and she introduced the boy to him. "This is Kennie Richards," she said. "How—how is Kathy? And Angelo, Mark? And what are you doing here alone, and not at the cabin?"

He had not seen her for almost two years, though she lived only in Boston. Two years! No, that was impossible. She had never gone away; she had always been with him, her voice in his ear, her face close to his. The girl sat down on the bench, and Mark sat down, too, and Kennie surveyed them with a shy smile. "Why don't you go down to the pond, dear?" asked Alice. "And here are the peanuts for the squirrels. Don't be long. You have the watch I gave you? Good. Be back in about fifteen minutes."

The boy went off, and Mark looked after him. Now, why couldn't he have had a son like that, with clear honest eyes, kind lips, and a face that expressed inner cleanliness? He had made no effort to charm; he had no coaxing and winning ways. A boy, a good boy.

Mark heard himself talking, and Alice replying, but it was some moments before he became conscious of what they were really saying. Alice was making her usual excuses for not visiting her family. She was very busy; she'd been getting her PhD. She was taking an advanced art course. She had many friends. Her classes were heavy, and she loved them all. She did not know where the time went. She had often planned . . .

She paused. Mark gazed at her calm profile, with its almost classic features. Alice was twenty-four now. The slight rigidity of expression that he remembered had disappeared. Her lips were softer, still sad, but with a brighter touch of color. She said, "I'm so happy for you and Kathy, Mark. I hope the baby will be a girl. I teach boys, of course, and I love them dearly, but I'd like to teach girls for a while. Kathy writes me the most buoyant and excited letters. Is she really as well as she sounds?"

"Yes, she's very well, and happy, Allie."

Alice paused again. "And—Angelo? How does he like the idea of a new brother or sister?"

"He doesn't know yet." Alice turned quickly on the bench and looked into his eyes, and they did not need to ask a question or form a reply.

"Kathy will tell him soon," said Mark at last. Dear Alice, dear clean Alice, with her decent look of integrity and pride, and all her unshakable dignity! He looked at the long neck, at the modest but well-fitting linen dress on her lovely figure, at her long quiet hands, at her smooth calves and delicate ankles. And then he could look no more and averted his face, and Alice saw his gray pallor, his thinness, the ashen streaks in his hair, his look of absolute exhaustion. She clenched her hands on her knees.

There were whole days together now, when she did not think of Mark. There were nights when she slept, and did not dream of him. There were occasions when she really enjoyed the company of other men; there was actually one young professor whom she was seriously considering marrying. And now, it was all gone, the hard-won peace, the tranquillity, the new life, the new hope, the feeling that her existence had not stopped and that she had not reached a blank wall in which there was not a door that could be opened on a fresh garden. It blew away like nothingness, and there was only Mark after all, and there had never been anyone else but Mark.

She bent her head and they sat in silence and stared sightlessly at the grass. Then with an effort Alice said, "You remember me talking about Kennie? I—I sent him to Miss Simmons' school, and I thought he liked it. And then he wouldn't go any longer, and he wouldn't tell me why. But he's going to a very nice new public school, with young teachers who are determined really to teach, and he's doing well and is happy." She hesitated. Did Mark know anything about what had happened to Kennie? But he had forgotten that she had ever spoken about him that summer day so long ago. He tried to listen with a show of interest. Alice sighed.

"When Jack and Mary are married the end of this month they are going to try to adopt Kennie," she said. "Jack McDowell. He says he often sees you. In fact, they have already put in an application. It will be wonderful for Kennie; he loves them both." She had thought that when she herself married she would adopt Kennie. But he was growing up; he needed a home of his own. And now her own hopes of being his adopted mother were gone forever.

"Yes," said Mark, in his listless voice. "Kathy and I are invited to the wedding, of course." He closed his eyes involuntarily. Something is terribly wrong, thought Alice, with alarm.

"Mark!" she cried. "Is something the matter? Is there anything I can do?"

"Allie," he said, not looking at her. "Why didn't you tell me that Angelo tried to kill you that day at the cabin?"

She put her hand quickly to her lips and looked at him with fear.

"You see," said Mark, "I went to Jack. I told him about—other occasions. I thought I was losing my mind for years. I wanted to believe that, honestly. I wanted to think I needed treatment or even confinement. Anything but the truth. And then, Jack told me the truth. He told me about you and Angelo, also."

"He shouldn't have! That was wrong!"

Mark shook his head. "No, Allie dear. It was right. If you had been the only—one—he wouldn't even have mentioned it, for kids sometimes do stupid and dangerous things out of impulse. But—there were the others, you see. And I went to Jack for help. And, he told me everything I would rather have died than hear."

Alice's face changed, became fixed as if in stone. "Mark," she almost whispered. "What are you saying? There were—other people?"

"Yes, Allie. And if you had told me the truth that day perhaps these others wouldn't have been hurt. I would have watched, just as I am watching now. Who knows, Allie,"—and out of his despair he wanted a sharing despair—"but that someone has been maimed, someone I haven't even heard of, someone I never even knew, an old man or a child or a woman, in an 'accident.' I'll never know. And it's my fault, and yours."

Alice began to cry, soundlessly, bending her head to hide the tears she could not stop. "I didn't tell you, Mark, I didn't want you to know. I was afraid it would hurt you too much."

He nodded like an automaton. "Yes, I understand that, I can understand that. I never told Kathy. I shouldn't have blamed you, Allie. Don't cry, please. Forgive me; I shouldn't have talked that way to you. But I've come to the end of something—I don't see how I can go on knowing my son is a dangerous psychopath, and that unless he is caught at some violence he'll never be taken away from others he can hurt. Jack tells me he is about to enter another stage of his development, and that he'll probably abandon even the slightest violence in the future. He'll be even more careful of himself than ever. But I begin to think of some little girl, somewhere, playing like those children around a pond, or in her backyard, or walking with her mother right now, perhaps, whom he'll marry. And I'm thinking of the children he'll have, and all the misery and despair he'll spread."

He struck his knee with his fist. "All the misery and the despair. It'll widen around him; he'll destroy his wife's happiness and love. His children will come to hate him; he'll make misfits and neurotics of them, and ruin their lives. He won't be able to help it. He is what he is. He can't be stopped or changed, no more than an elemental force, or a storm. You know there's nothing to appeal to, except his own welfare, and he'll take care of that very well out in the world which can either hate or love him! Yes. And serve him, too. Sometimes, Allie, I wish he'd get out of control, really out of control, and do something, something frightful which he can't hide, and then, perhaps, there will be a place for him and he'll be locked away safely."

Alice could not bear the anguish in his voice, the stifled breathing she heard. She put her hand on Mark's arm, and tightened her fingers around it. She was horrified at its emaciation.

"He used to have such awful rages," the girl stammered. "But Kathy writes me that now he seldom loses his temper, hardly more than once a month, and he's easier to calm. Perhaps we can hope a little."

Mark shook his head again. "His rages are fewer, yes, and sometimes he gets over them quicker; he doesn't throw or smash things as he used to do. But he looks wild and mad when he is in a rage, Alice, not with a child's wildness and madness, but a man's. I don't care what Jack says, Alice. Angelo's insane when he's in a rage. I can still take hold of him forcibly, and hold him until he subsides. But the day will come when he will be too big and too strong. What then?"

"But Jack," said Alice insistently, "has said he'll control himself better and better as he grows older—for his own sake. You must hope, Mark!"

"For what?" he said drearily. "For the day I die? That's all I have to look forward to. And always, I'll have to watch Angelo until he's a man, and has left home, and then I'll just be waiting, waiting for any day—"

"Don't, Mark!" she cried. "You've forgotten. Kathy is going to have another child! Think of that child, Mark. I know it will be a wonderful child, and that it will make you happy, and help you to forget Angelo."

He sat, slumped, on the bench and looked at his crossed ankles. And then Kennie Richards was there, concerned at what he saw. He went to Alice and put his hand on her shoulder, and she tried to smile at him, but could only sob.

Kennie had known who Mark was from the moment of introduction, but with his kind subtlety he had also known that Alice did not want him to identify himself as a former classmate of Angelo's. He turned his sorrowful and understanding eyes on Mark, as he stood with his hand on Alice's shoulder, and some intuition told him that they had been speaking of Angelo Saint, and were devastated in consequence.

Alice rose, brushing away her tears. "I have a train to make in less than two hours," she said. "And I have to take Kennie home first. His foster parents will be worried about him; they moved back into the City, so I won't have to take him far. Mark," she added, "did you hear what I said?"

He looked up at her from the depths of his gray agony, and then got to his feet. "Alice," he said, "I wish you'd visit us. I wish you'd come, sometime."

"I will," she replied. "I honestly will. I expect to be with Kathy when the baby is born in October."

He watched the tall girl and the tall boy walk away together, and it seemed to him that only they were real and that his wife and his son were half-remembered dreams without reality. He went back to his lonely house. He was not hungry. He made a large drink for himself, and then sat in the gathering darkness until the whiskey quieted him. Then he took another drink, and then another, in a sort of frenzy, until he slept, stupefied.

CHAPTER THIRTEEN

Jack McDowell had told Mark Saint that psychopaths were absolutely unable to feel any deep and genuine emotion of love or liking for anyone but themselves. All their apparent life-serving virtues and sympathies were imitated, their love, facile though it was, was given but to those who could serve, flatter or be of value. But, Jack had said, there was as much difference among psychopaths as there was among all other natures. Some were homicidal, and these were responsible for a series, over a long period of time, of secret inexplicable murders committed for no apparent reason, not even for gain. Some were afflicted with paranoia, and in consequence were suspicious and hostile and incorrigible, never making the synthetic adjustment to society that the more intelligent of their kind accomplished, for their intelligence was inferior. Some never physically injured anyone in their lives; their attacks on others were mental and spiritual, with a complete refinement of cruelty. Some suddenly so lost all control of themselves—and absence of control when feeling one of their few genuine emotions, rage, was typical of them—that they committed mass murders in their berserk frenzy, and often within a short period of time. "Such as that seventeen-year-old-boy in Philadelphia, recently, who got a gun somewhere and killed five people whom he had never seen before, in as many minutes." Some were actually insane, but no more than in any other group.

But all were distinguished by a passionate narcissism, a monstrous and overwhelming vanity, and by an eternal watchfulness that that vanity was never threatened and that their power over others was never diminished. Keep the average psychopath assured of unswerving adoration, convinced that not only was he in the very center of his own world but in the very center of others, and he was comparatively harmless except to those who helplessly loved him. There, he was ruthless; there he spared no exploitation; there he had not even a superficial pity; there, he exerted all his power for delicate torture. Oppose him never—and this was true of all psychopaths—except when showing him that it was to his material or immediate benefit. Psychopaths were raw cynics.

"I would say," Jack had stated, "that perhaps all infants are partial psychopaths in their way, but as they grow into childhood their moral nature, endowed by God, begins to assert itself. This never happens in the true psychopath."

When exposed by others for what they were, they were never ashamed. They were only monstrously affronted and outraged; they never forgave. They waited for their opportunity to avenge the insult to themselves. For the intelligent psychopath was quite aware he was not like other men; this did not embarrass him or cause him any guilt. For he always considered himself the superior one, who must never be scorned or reviled, judged by the standards of others, or expected, in his emotions, to be as contemptibly "soft" and stupid and weak as others. He was, above all else, his own law.

"Would you say it was infantilism?" Mark had asked.

"No. Many people retain infantile traits, such as dependence, bad temper, weakness, constant demands to be assured that they are loved, resentment of authority and responsibility, without being at all psychopathic. If you mean infantilism only in the sense that some are atavists, born without a moral sense and conscience, throwbacks, then that is an entirely different thing." He added, "Infantile people can often become comparatively adult, and they are capable of real and genuine love and emotional concern for others, and often feel guilty, honestly guilty. And they can often rise to heights of self-abnegation, to the astonishment of others. These are not true of the psychopath. It is an odd thing, too—infantile people frequently become alcoholics. Psychopaths rarely do, for they want, at all times, to be in command of their power over others. But, I warn you: it is very hard to detect a psychopath;

sometimes even the best of psychiatrists can't do it, for they're very clever and their disguise is almost perfect and they have learned the jargon of normality."

"And there is no doubt that Angelo is a psychopath?"

"None whatever. I've told you he is the prototype of them all. I've never seen a better specimen, if you want to call it 'better.' "

So Mark, in his talks with his son when Kathy was not present, urged improvement in some overt behavior, "because you don't want people to think you're stupid or foolish, do you, Angelo? You—you have to deceive people; they're easy to deceive, and when you deceive them you can get what you want from them. You understand?"

Angelo, at those moments, admired "the old man." Perhaps he wasn't as stupid as he, Angelo, believed. He did not know that Mark hated himself for this gross materialism which he did not believe in for a moment; he hated himself for being a part of Angelo's crafty and astute cynicism and self-serving—for the sake not only of the boy but of others.

Sometimes, in his stricken despair, Mark wanted to cry out against all caution and advice: "I'm lying to you! The man who serves only himself has no right to live among human beings; he has no right to be a part of the human community! The man who exploits others, without mercy or guilty compassion, is a tiger, and should be destroyed! The man without God is a fierce animal, and should be exiled as they once exiled lepers, for he is a spiritual leper!" But he always restrained himself. He knew that a sly and amused amber gleam would come to Angelo's eyes, and that Angelo would completely despise him, and that his danger to others would become stronger. For, though Angelo might say, as he said when he was younger, and with demureness, "Yes, Daddy," he would not understand a single word, and what little real influence his father had over him would be lost.

One late July weekend Mark came to the cabin to see his family. It had been very hot all these weeks; Kathy had decided it was best for Angelo not to return to the City as they usually did, coming to the cabin only for the weekends. "We'll have an extra month, darling, though we'll miss you," she said to Mark, on whom she was leaning these days. "But you can come up every weekend; after all, it isn't far. Besides, I do feel so good and lively up here."

She did not drive her own car any longer, but Betty, the placid maid, could drive, and could go down to the village for replacements of food and supplies. Sometimes Kathy and Angelo would go with her. Angelo stayed very close to his mother; there was some threat, somewhere, his preternatural senses told him, and he watched his mother sharply. But she was more loving than ever, more sedulous. It was only that sometimes she had a dreaming expression in her eyes, and a slight, faraway smile, which Angelo suspected did not concern him. These were infrequent, but enough to alert his powerful animal senses.

The family was to return to the suburb this Sunday night, Betty following in Kathy's car, for it was time for the periodic examination and attention to Angelo's teeth before the new term of school began. On Wednesday, Kathy and Angelo and Betty would go back to the cabin.

"You've got to tell him this time, Kathy!" said Mark, on Sunday. "Even your skirts and your elastic waistbands aren't going to conceal the truth much longer."

"I'll tell him after I see the doctor; don't be so fussy, Mark dear," said Kathy. "I just can't wait! I can just see him jumping for joy! And excitement!"

"Kathy," said Mark, "will you promise me not to tell him unless I am there?"

Kathy looked at him quickly. "Why, what a funny expression you have, Mark! Why should I wait?"

"I've told you a dozen times," he answered, with weariness, "and it never penetrates. Look. The baby is my baby, too; I'd like to have a share in the telling. And, in another way, childbearing is a woman's world, and Angelo is a boy. He'll be confused; he might even be resentful. That's normal, in older children; they don't want to feel displaced. Now wait, Kathy. I know you'll assure him he'll never be displaced. But he'll understand that he'll have to share your love and your time and devotion, and that's a jolt to any child. I want to be present, as a man, as a member of his own sex, to give him some moral support. Can't you understand?"

"All right," said Kathy grudgingly, and with disappointment. She had envisaged a loving, secret session with her son, holding him in her arms, confiding her hopes to him, petting him, being petted in return by her "little man." And now Mark was spoiling it! He was really very selfish. But she understood to a certain extent; after all, Mark was the father. Perhaps Mark, too, was feeling in advance another displacement in his wife's affection. She suddenly smiled at her husband, nodded, and patted his arm. All men were still boys!

Kathy was careful not to let Angelo know the name of the obstetrician she was visiting. He was so intelligent! He would know almost at once. As for his going with her, and seeing potential mothers in various stages of bloat, that would be embarrassing to her. So, on Monday morning, she said to him, "Darling, you must take a taxi to your dentist this afternoon. Betty is going to drive me to my doctor's—"

Angelo's eyes widened. "But you were at the doctor's only a month ago!"

"Yes, dear. But the tests aren't—aren't complete—"

He was frightened. Did she have cancer or some other mortal disease, which would remove her from his life forever? Or diabetes? There had been a boy in his class who had had diabetes; he had died! The old lady was looking fat and flabby recently, just as that boy had looked. Angelo's fear ripened to real terror. If his mother died, then the old man would soon comfort himself! He'd bring that ugly and vicious Aunt Alicia here! He'd marry her! And then—and then— Angelo, in unaffected horror, threw himself upon Kathy so that she reeled under his weight. His eyes flooded with tears; he turned white.

"You've got to tell me!" he screamed. "What's the matter with you? What tests? For what?" He saw Alice in this house, stern Alice with her eyes which saw everything, who remembered that he had tried to kill her. She would send him away to that damned military school. She would be afraid to have him here; she would deprive him of all that he enjoyed. She hated him. His life would be over, all his pleasant, adulation-surrounded life, all his luxuries, all the pamperings, all the devotion, all the pocket-money, all the privileges. His mind blazed with his furious and terrified thoughts, his dark horrors. Alice, when married to his father, would tell him everything; women always told their husbands, the idiots. And then, it could even be confinement in some locked place! His beautiful face was convulsed. He stamped; he shrieked; he wept; he tore up and down the room.

And Kathy looked at him and her heart melted, and her eyes swam with adoring tears. The darling, the darling, the darling! Her heart's own love. He was afraid for her; he was frightened that she was ill; he was full of fear of losing her! He was a little man, wanting to protect her. And she held out her foolish arms to him, and he struck them aside in his panic.

Now he was running faster up and down the room, like a caged beast, uttering the wildest and most savage of desperate cries. "No, no!" he bellowed hoarsely. "No! No! I can't stand it! I won't stand it!"

And he saw Alice standing before him, unmoved, hating, loathing, and his father beside her with a changed cold face, condemning him, accusing him, pushing him away. Perhaps men would come with a straitjacket, intoning, "We know all about you; we know all about you. You tried to kill your aunt. You tried to hurt or kill Jane Whythe; you drove Kennie Richards from your school. You tripped—you injured—you hurt—all those others. All those others no one knows about but us. And now we've got you. We'll take you away and you'll live in a cell—"

Hateful, stupid, goddam fools! They'd never understand! They wouldn't even listen to his explanations. They wouldn't know that he'd had to remove those people from his way, that they frustrated or laughed at or defied him or disliked him or knew all about him!

The frenzied thoughts calmed a little. Perhaps he was exaggerating. He stopped in the center of the room, panting. His head hurt; his heart tumbled in his chest. Kathy, still holding out her arms, was a pinkish blur to him in her pretty blue bedroom. Only his thoughts, his conjectures, were real. Mark might send him away to a military school: he would! There was no doubt of it, for Alice would not have him here. But he wouldn't be sent to—a cell, or something. After all, that idiot father of his was still his father. But a military school! The discipline, the conformity, the demanded obedience, the treating of all boys like all others! The disgusting uniforms! The regulations! And there were men there, not easily deceived women, not soft, weak women who could be cajoled and deceived. Angelo, when first he had heard mention of a military school, had enlightened himself about them by discreet questions, by studying books in the library. He had seen the photographs of the kind of retired soldiers who ruled such schools, uncompromising, quietly disillusioned, quietly strong and comprehending men. They would know all about him, these broad-shouldered, firm-chinned, clear-eyed men. They would especially be warned about him by Alice and his father.

Deceitful and cruel himself, it was impossible for him to believe that others were not like that, also. Oh, he understood that there were only two kinds of people in the world: the eating and the eaten! The soft, weak, whimpering ones; the harsh and taking and merciless ones! There were no other kinds. But all, even the weakest and most timid, were devourers.

Only one person stood between him and the unspeakable future, and that was his mother. And she was sick; she might even be dying. He ran to her, his face awash with genuine tears, his usually rosy cheeks white and drawn.

"You've got to tell me!" he screamed. "Right now! You've got to tell me! I can't wait until you come back from the doctor!" And he stamped his foot violently. He seized her arm again; he shook her with great strength.

"What's wrong?" he shrieked. "Do you have cancer, or something? Are you going to leave me?" He was freshly affrighted by her soft, moved face, by her trembling lips, by her tears. All her features seemed to be melting together in one quiver. She began to sob. She tried to take him into her arms. She was touched as she had never been touched before, and her adoration for her son reached the heights of blasphemous worship. Seeing all this, Angelo felt faint for the first time in his robust life; sweat appeared on his forehead, on his upper lip, spread under his white shirt.

Again, he flung her reaching arms aside, and sprang back from her. If Kathy had not been so unbearably moved, so trembling with joy and love and worship, so overwhelmed by the sight of what she believed to be her son's fear for her, his terror for her, his grief for her, even she would have been stopped by his awful expression, which was not the expression of a child. Even she, the fatuous mother, would have retreated under the fire of those terrible eyes, and she might have fled, understanding that here was no loving child, no son, but a monster. She would have recognized an insane and murderous rage when she saw it, a rage inspired by self-love. And, in an eruption of the instinct for self-preservation, she would have run for help, screaming, down the stairs, dreading to hear, in her panic, the following footsteps, the awful face, of a murderer.

But Kathy was overwhelmed. She wiped her eyes; she sobbed softly, with rapture, with ecstasy, that this darling of hers, this adorable son, loved her so passionately. There were fools who warned of pampering children too much, of coddling them, of giving them everything they wished, of elevating them in their own estimations too much, of pouring endless love and devotion upon them! If only they could see her darling now, so white, so frightened for her! Then they, too, would bow their heads humbly before The Children.

Then Kathy thought suddenly, I can't bear for him to be so upset, so afraid. Why should any adult let a child hang in suspense, and imagine all kinds of fearful things? It's cruel, cruel. If I keep my promise to Mark, God knows what my darling will suffer until Mark comes home tonight, and we tell Angel together! How can I do that to the very core of my heart? I'd be a dreadful kind of mother, and I'd never forgive myself.

Angel, all at once, was ominously quiet. He listened with his inner ear. His mother was holding a debate with herself; he knew that delicate nibbling of her lower lip with her small white teeth; he knew that silly glow in her eyes, that secret, delighted smile. He knew the arch expression, the radiant look. He stood and watched her; his heart was still roaring; his breath was still heavy and audible. But he was waiting now.

And then, Kathy was lifting her right forefinger archly; she was cocking her head; she was preening. He knew the signs. She had a secret, and she was going to impart it to him. It wasn't a dangerous secret, it wasn't something that threatened him. Or was it?

He watched her as she tiptoed elaborately about the room, preparing to divulge the delicious secret. Angelo became puzzled, and more wary than ever. He knew all these disgusting symptoms, which he had endured indulgently in the past, for it usually meant something delightful about to happen to him. She locked the door with dainty, flourishing gestures; she peeked into her blue and pink bathroom as though, idiot! she thought some one was hiding there who should not hear what she was about to say. She ran to the window, and carefully pulled aside the draperies, and peeped outside. Idiot! Fool! Stupid, fat old woman! Yes, she was getting fat and shapeless; she ate too much. And she was old, old and revolting. He winced and clenched his teeth at the sound of her ruffled lace petticoats under the bouncing, foolish skirt. He shivered at the sight of her profile, girlish, naughtily sly, grinning, as she looked through the window. Her auburn curls were in rings around her flushed cheeks and wizened neck.

And then she hugged herself with a girlish trill. "Betty's out in the garden, cutting the last roses, and some phlox!" she caroled. "Oh, we'll have such a celebration tonight! There'll even be a teentsy glass of wine for my darling, to toast! How we'll laugh together, and plan! Oh, oh, I can't wait!"

Stupid old bitch! What was she talking about? But Angelo's eyes lost their fire, and began to sparkle with anticipation. This must be a special occasion. There were no birthdays imminent. There were no anniversaries at hand. It must be very special. But why did she always have to go through this babyish ritual, this mincing, this self-hugging, this trilling, this radiance? Angelo's heart still thudded, but it was quieter. Still, he felt that he would shout, maddened beyond endurance, after what he had just suffered, by this imbecility of his mother's. What was there he wanted? A treehouse he had been coaxing for up at the cabin? A motor bike, which his father had forbidden? A motor scooter, even more quickly forbidden? Angelo caught his breath. He had talked winningly of that motor scooter only yesterday; several of the boys at school had them; his father had not exactly said no this time. He had merely frowned and answered nothing. A motor scooter! Angelo forgot all about his mother's impending visit to the doctor. She would not be so flushed now, so delighted, so arch, so coquettish, if there was anything serious in the background. She looked well, even if she was so damned fat lately, with bulging breasts.

She tiptoed over to Angelo, teetering, smiling, clapping her hands. He was almost as tall as she, yet she bent in her silly way as if he were two years old.

"Guess!" she sang. "Oh, my darling, guess!"

Angelo, through the open window, filled with sun, could hear the brisk clipping of Betty's garden shears in the hot silence. He could hear sudden locusts whirr. There was no other sound.

He was still unnerved. But he controlled himself. "There—there isn't anything wrong with you, Mum?" he asked, thinking of the doctor again. "I mean, you wanting to have more tests—"

"Oh, no, no! In fact, I was never better in my life, sweetheart. Never better! Never happier! Oh, my sweet, and you were worried so about your mother—" She stretched out her hand to ruffle his crisp curls, but he drew back. He breathed a heavy sigh of relief. His face began to shine. It was something special for him, something wonderful for him. She had been going today to order it; she had been lying; she had not intended to go to the doctor at all. He smiled like the sun.

"A motor bike? A motor scooter?" he said lovingly. "I can't wait. Tell me."

"Oh, oh, oh!" cried Kathy in rapture. "Much, much more wonderful than that! So wonderful that sometimes I can't believe it! And I just can't wait, though I promised your father not to tell you! It's naughty of me, but I just can't wait!"

He began to sweat, now, with glorious anticipation. What? What?

"You'll dance with joy!" sang Kathy. "We'll dance together!"

Angelo, in his consuming curiosity, wanted to slap her. His heart was thumping again. And there she was, tiptoeing, wetting her lips with her tongue, grinning like a half-wit, swishing her skirts, and moving, high step after exaggerated high step, towards one of her large fruit-wood dressers. And then, dramatically, she pulled open one of the larger drawers. "Come and see for yourself, Angel. Come and feast your eyes yourself!"

He flew across the room. Holding his breath, he looked into the drawers. They were heaped with infants' clothing, tiny white dresses trimmed with lace, minute shirts, fluffy little coats, bonnets, doll-like stockings, blankets, fluffy petticoats, diapers.

Angelo fell back. His face turned a curious doughy color; his lips thickened; his eyes dilated. He was so stunned that he could not speak or move. He watched his mother lovingly touch those loathsome things; he saw her lift a shirt and kiss it and hold it against her rosy cheek; he saw her pressing a small white shoe against her lips. And he knew. He knew without a single doubt.

And then, as Kathy, her back to him, began that murmurous litany of adoration he knew so well—but which was not for him, now!—and he saw the kisses, the love, the fondling, he was filled with the most appalling rage he had ever experienced, the most overpowering of hatreds, the most tearing of furies. Everything enlarged in the room, tilted, became outlined with a rippling of flame. The top of his head was a lid of red-hot iron, hammering onto his naked brain. He could not breathe. He began to shudder; the insane light in the room brightened, glowed, flamed, until it was the breath of a cauldron.

Yet his thoughts, though appalled, were orderly enough. There was going to be a baby. A boy, or a girl. There was going to be another center of adoration, another deity. There was going to be a rival, another point of attention. There was going to be someone else to share every thought of his parents, every loving touch of his mother's, all her pampering. There would be another bed to visit. There would be another voice to which his mother would listen, another hand she would lead to delights, another creature who would demand. Something shifted in the boy; he felt an invisible pushing for place inside yet outside him. He felt a dreadful struggling for power. This was something he could not endure; this was something he would not endure, he dared not endure! All that he had, all that he was, was mortally threatened! He was undone; he had become only another member of the family, and not its absolute center. Someone else would take his place, someone younger—No, no, no! he shrieked in himself. No!

No other threat, however formidable, had been so terrible, so imminent, so certain as this for him. Always, he had overcome the threat, removed it, destroyed it, frightened it away, intimidated or deceived it into acquiescence. But he could do none of these things to the invisible peril in his mother's body, the absolute peril, the titanic peril. He was helpless. He had often heard his parents discussing his "inheritance," as they called it, when he listened slyly at their door. A lot of money! It belonged to him. And now it would not belong to him alone. He would have only part of it. There would be somebody else, somebody as yet faceless, yet equal to him, perhaps someone more powerful than he, displacing him, driving him away, rendering him insignificant in its infant might.

He had been most horribly, most deliberately, betrayed! His parents together had done this to him, in the darkness of some loathsome night. He had not, after all, had them completely in the palms of his hands; he had not, after all, been the undisputed center of their lives! They had done this to him! They had dared to do this thing to him! For months, now, they had humored him, and all the time they had been laughing at him, he, Angelo Saint! Did they, after all, honestly expect that he'd stand for it? Did they think that what they had done to him would go unpunished?

Kathy was cooing over some lace-trimmed, infant nightgowns, her face transfigured as she thought of the coming child. She shook out a gown; she laughed softly; she kissed the glossy folds. A little girl, perhaps, to be adored also, to be pampered and petted by herself and Mark and dearest Angelo! What fun they would have with her! What joy over her first tooth, her first step, her first laugh and smile! Kathy's arms ached for the child six months in her womb, three months away! How could they all wait that long?

Watching her, Angelo cringed and shuddered and hated her beyond anyone else he had ever hated. His thoughts rolled like a sparkling wheel. He had only to wait until the baby was born, the usurper, the betrayer. No! That would be too long.

Kathy replaced the garments with the tenderest hands, looked at them long and with passion, and closed the drawer as if closing it on a beloved face. She then glanced up at the mirror over the dresser. And she saw Angelo's face reflected in it.

Her hands remained in the air, paralyzed. Her breath stopped in her throat. Her heart gave a great bound. For never had she seen his face like this, mature, distorted, disfigured by hate, murderous. She could not believe it! She continued to stare at it; a throb of pain flashed across her forehead, and there was a sudden roiling sickness in her stomach. The child in her womb, feeling her perturbation perhaps, moved restlessly. What's the matter with Angel? thought Kathy, with confusion.

She swung about quickly. But as quickly as she swung he as quickly controlled his features; he was an expert in these matters. He was very white, but his face was calm. Oh! thought Kathy. It was only an effect of glass and light! But she continued to feel weak and ill.

"Angel!" she exclaimed. She felt for her chair and sat down in it, and tried to smile. Her instincts were alive and clamoring in her, but she suppressed them. The soft summer wind blew out the curtains a little; Betty was snipping closer to the house. She was singing tunelessly. A distant dog barked.

Angelo moved very softly toward his mother and stood near her.

"You're old, Mum," he said seriously. "You'll die if you have this—baby."

Kathy forced a difficult smile, her eyes on his face, her eyes remembering, but her mind repudiating.

"Oh no, dear. The doctor said I am in excellent health. In fact, I am due at his office in less than an hour; Betty's driving me." Why was there a sharp pain like a knife in her throat? "Lots of women, much older than I am, have babies without trouble. You—you mustn't worry your dear, darling head about me."

The fury boiled up in Angelo again, but he restrained

it. The strange and flickering outline was still around every
object, as if it were on fire.

"Why didn't you stop it—when it began?" he asked.

Kathy heard, but refused to hear it with her mind.
"What do you mean, dear?" she faltered.

"There was a boy in our class. His sister got into
trouble; everybody knew about it, and we laughed. It was
their chauffeur. She was going to marry him. Her father
stopped it. And they took her away for an operation, and
that was the end of the baby." He made fists of his hands.
His voice rose thinly, again almost a shriek. "Why didn't
you stop it like that?"

Kathy put her hands quickly to the sides of her face
and stared at him. She swallowed a few times, unable to
speak. Oh, this was not Angel, this stranger with the
terrible eyes, this stranger who had said such terrible
things! This was not her baby speaking.

"You could have stopped it!" he wailed. "Why did you
have to do this to me? Why, why? What've I ever done to
you? I tried—I tried—and now you've done it!"

He looked at her collapsed body in the chair; the foolish
skirt was pulled tight across it, and he saw that her belly
was swollen. How soon would the Terror be born, the
usurper? Four months? Three months? Two?

Kathy swallowed over and over. Her throat and mouth
were like paper, dry and choking. She put a hand to her
breast.

Then a radiant smile broke out on her face. She understood! Of course! Hadn't Mark told her, and the doctor
too, and Alice in her letters? Silly she! She hadn't listened,
but it was true! The older child was always jealous, at
first, of his prerogatives, always afraid that he would be
displaced in his parents' affections, always had to be
reassured and told that no other child would ever take his
place. Poor child. The dear Children, The Children, The
Children! It was very natural, and Angelo was the most
natural and normal boy in the world, going on eleven
now, able to understand—but still just a child. Of course
he was a little resentful and jealous. It only had to be
explained to him, he need only be given extra love and
reassurance. Kathy forgot the glimpse she had had of her

son's awful face; she forgot what he had just said. She held out her arms to him.

"Oh, darling, you're just jealous!" she trilled with girlish delight. "Come to Mum, dear. Here, sit right here on the edge of my knee, and I'll have a nice cozy chat with you. I'll explain. Did you think for a minute that anyone, even this lovely, lovely baby, would take your place in our hearts? Why, each child has his own special place in the hearts of his parents—no one can take it away from him. Look, I have five fingers on my hand, and each one is different and each one is necessary. If I lost one of them, would the others take its place? No, no!"

Angelo's face had become smooth and bland as it always did when he was thinking and plotting, and Kathy thought that he was listening to her, that she had comforted him and dispelled his "jealousy." She giggled with happiness. She stood up and again held out her arms to her son.

Angelo let her come the right distance. He measured it carefully. And then, while Kathy stood before him, a big wide smile on her unsuspecting face, her arms outstretched to take and embrace him, he lifted his large foot deliberately and kicked his mother accurately, strongly, powerfully, in the very center of her living belly, where the usurper was, where the Terror crouched, waiting to be born to deprive him, but where it would now die, where it must die.

So violent was the blow that Kathy, her face becoming absolutely blank with shock, staggered back. Before she could regain her balance, Angelo kicked her precisely and even more powerfully in the same spot.

Kathy, her face still blank, her eyes still staring witlessly, reeled. She flung out her arms to stop herself from falling. She caught the back of her dressing-table chair. For one nightmare moment she appeared to dance with it, and then it toppled with her weight and she fell upon it, sprawling.

It was then she uttered a dreadful animal cry of agony, of purely physical agony. She uttered it over and over, and Betty, in the garden below, heard it and was stunned and paralyzed, the scissors in her hand, the cut flowers all about her.

Angelo came close to his mother, lying there like a broken doll over the chair. He said, through his teeth, "That'll teach you you can't do this to me! It's all your fault!" he suddenly cried. "It's all your fault! You made me do it!"

The empty eyes looked up at him, and then the soul of Kathy knew. She did not scream again. She only lay on the back of the chair, the legs thrusting against her body. In falling, she had hit her lip; it was bleeding profusely. She was not aware of it; she was not aware of the convulsions of agony in her body. She could only look at her son, the murderer.

The door slammed below, and there was a frightened call. Angelo, half-crouching, wheeled. But he knew what he had to do. He screamed, shouted, "My mother! My mother!" he howled. "Come and help Mum! I don't know what to do!"

He ran out of the room. Betty had reached the dimly shining hall below, and she was running toward the staircase. Crying wildly, Angelo ran to the head of the stairs and prepared to descend toward her, still screaming about his mother who had "fallen down."

Betty, standing aghast below, did not know exactly what happened. Did the boy's foot catch on a minutely loose carpet seam? Did he stumble? Did he trip on his own feet? Had his false tears blinded him? No one would ever know.

But as Betty stood stonelike, unable to move, she saw his large body lift itself in the air like a bird on the top of the long stairway. He soared, and then he struck halfway down. But the impetus was too great. He bounced and lifted again, and turned over and over. And then, with a nauseating crash he plunged almost directly at Betty's feet, and landed full on his head on the marble floor.

CHAPTER FOURTEEN

Mark Saint sat in the waiting room with Alice Knowles beside him. They had sat this way for three hideous days, praying silently to themselves, hoping against hope. But only Alice wept. Mark's eyes remained stiff and dry and staring. The nurses looked at him with pity; the doctors came to him often, begging him to go home to rest. He would not leave. He had taken a room in the hospital to be near his wife, who was dying, who could not possibly live with her internal injuries. So the doctors had told him. They had not told him something else: that Kathy was making no effort to live, that she had lost the will to live. They looked into her dulling eyes, and they knew. Yet she had not been told that her son was dead, that he had died instantly of a crushed skull.

And Kathy was mute. She lay like one already dead, and suffered her husband's kisses, and Alice's. She did not speak; sometimes she moaned and groaned speechlessly, especially in her drugged sleep. But she did not speak.

The baby, born prematurely, had been dead, desperately injured in Kathy's "fall." It was a beautiful little girl. Even the nurses had cried over its pretty perfection, and had handled the small body tenderly.

The police had questioned Betty minutely. The tearful girl had nothing much to tell them. She had been in the garden. She thought she had heard a thump. And then Mrs. Saint was screaming, over and over. She had run into the house, and was preparing to climb up the stairs when Angelo had appeared. She repeated what he had shrieked. His mother had fallen; he was calling to Betty to help her. And then he had plunged down the stairs, right before her. He had died before the doctor she had frantically

169

summoned had arrived. They had found Mrs. Saint unconscious on the top of her boudoir chair, and had taken her at once to the hospital.

The police, who knew all about psychopaths, had had their suspicions of Betty. But her background was impeccable; they even inspected her school records. They had asked neighbors and Mark and friends if Betty had ever shown any hostility toward any of the Saints. One "interviewer," at the police station, had actually been a psychiatrist, unknown to Betty. He had said that not only was she absolutely sane and normal, but that she was honestly grief-stricken over the tragedy. In fact, he had to put her under sedation. She had cried over and over, "Oh, if I hadn't left her! But she sent me out to cut flowers! But she was always so gay. She was in such good health; she was awfully careful, but she moved around like a young girl. Oh, poor Mrs. Saint, poor woman, poor Angelo!" She was beside herself with sorrow. Sometimes, incoherently, she blamed herself. If she just hadn't obeyed Mrs. Saint and left her alone, with only the boy in the house! It was only for a few minutes, but she shouldn't have left her! It took many days of the psychiatrist's best efforts to remove the awful weight of guilt from Betty's heart. It took even longer for her priest to reassure her that it had all been an Act of God, and that she could not have prevented it. But still, the burden of grief remained with Betty for six months, long after she had gone home to her relatives in the City.

It was only Dr. McDowell who had the darkest and faintest of suspicions, and he never told them even to Alice. Once he had asked the stricken Mark, "Of course, it doesn't matter now, but did your wife ever tell the boy she was to have a baby?" And Mark had replied in a lifeless voice, "No. But she was going to tell him that night; we were going to have a family celebration when we told him. She'd promised me . . ."

Just the darkest and faintest of suspicions. Jack had examined Kathy, the day after the tragedy. Was that a broad heel-mark on her belly? Or was it the mark of the chair-leg when she had fallen over the chair? Her skirts had been thick and full, not enough to save her child, but thick enough to blur the outlines of the hemorrhaging great bruise on her flesh. Yes, Jack had his ghastly suspicions. But what good would it do to voice them now, even to the family physician? The murderer—if Angelo had actually and inadvertently murdered his mother in the attempt to kill the unborn child—was dead. Any further examination or talk would only arouse Mark's own suspicions, and his life would be ruined forever. Better to leave it this way. Better to let Angelo's grave bury what had truly happened.

And, of course, Kathy was saying nothing. When she had recovered consciousness in the hospital, after her baby had been born dead, the police had asked her only a few gentle questions. She had said, so faintly they had hardly heard, "I—fell. That's all. I fell."

There was one eloquent thing that confirmed Jack McDowell's suspicions, but seemed not to arouse the suspicions of others. Kathy never asked for Angelo. She did not know he was dead. She had not heard him fall. But— she never asked for him.

"I'm glad she doesn't," Mark said to his friend. "But then, she's so heavily drugged, isn't she? She probably just thinks he's safe at home."

"Yes," said Jack. "That's it, of course." He paused. "If she ever does ask about him—just say that you don't want him to know how sick his mother is, and that you've sent him back to the cabin, with Betty."

But Kathy never asked. She rarely spoke. But she wanted Mark with her every moment that she was awake. She would lie absolutely still, her chill hand in his, and would only fix her simple eyes on his face. A very few times a tear would run down her cheek, to Mark's heartbreak. She not only did not ask for Angelo, she did not speak of the child she had lost, either.

Sometimes Alice, who relieved Mark, would look at her sister and she would feel that her own heart was crushed. Poor Kathy! Poor children, the one who had died, the one who had been killed in his headlong fall. There were moments when she forgave Angelo. There were moments when she could grieve for him. He had been so exceptionally beautiful and charming and intelligent. Perhaps a miracle might have happened, in spite of what Jack had once said. Perhaps he might have become truly human in time.

The funeral had been quiet and private. Angelo's body had been laid in the family plot. And very soon, if the doctors were right, Kathy would lie beside him forever, with her baby's body at her feet. Poor Kathy. Alice's tears were like burning acid in her eyes, and she reproached herself over and over that she had ever been impatient with that loving and fatuous mother. But Mark was her worst suffering, Mark with his haggard blank face, Mark with his dry and unseeing eyes. She sat beside him, with no words of consolation—for such words were foolish— but she prayed silently for him.

Kathy hardly breathed in her high narrow bed, with the sun streaming through the window, its pleasant curtains floating. Sometimes her nurses bent over her suddenly and sharply, to see if she were still alive, and felt her pulse. She lay flaccid; sometimes her open eyes would stare blankly at the ceiling, and Alice would wonder if she were truly conscious and thinking of anything at all. Hour by hour her face dwindled, became smaller, and hour by hour her glazed eyes sank back into her skull.

It was Alice who was alone with her on the fourth midnight when she died.

The nurse had stepped out "for a moment." Mark was resting, exhausted, in his room. The night light was on, a vague softness. Alice was beside the bed, watching her sister. Kathy's eyes were half open; she was breathing a little quickly. Alice bent over her anxiously. Kathy's face was covered with great drops of cold sweat. Then her eyes turned fully on Alice and she recognized her sister, and she smiled a little.

"Alicia," she murmured.

"Sleep, dear," said Alice, and swallowed her tears.

Kathy moved her head restlessly; her eyes had a fixed look, far and quietly terrible. "Not yet," she murmured. "I just want to say something. I think I knew—all the time, even when he was a baby. But I used to read—the books, you know, about child care. There was one doctor—he called children "petals and flowers.' And—somebody wrote there weren't any bad children, just bad parents. No. No! It isn't true! The Bible is right—about man being wicked from his birth and evil from his youth. Most of us—dear—we learn better because we are better. But—others—like—like—"

She paused. Her breath came faster. A look of absolute terror and grief stood on her face. The great drops on her face glittered in the night light, and she clutched Alice's hand.

"The others—they don't have souls. Not like ours, never. That's why they kill, and do—other things—and we can't believe they're what they are—"

Kathy panted. She even tried to raise herself on her pillows in her desperate urgency to communicate, speaking rapidly with her last strength.

"They think I don't—know—that he's dead! I do! I prayed that he'd die, since I was brought here! And—and this morning—I knew. It—it is such a consolation; Mark won't suffer anymore. Be good to him—be good to him—"

Her eyes closed. Her breath stopped. She died between one moment and another.

EPILOGUE

A year and a half later Jack McDowell sat with Mark Saint in his apartment in the City. Alice, who had prepared the dinner they had just enjoyed, was clearing away the dishes in the kitchen with the help of Jack's pretty wife, Mary. Mark had long ago sold his house in the suburbs; he had never returned there after that day of tragedy except to remove his belongings.

The two men puffed together contentedly in the December dusk. The sounds of the City came to them muffled and agreeable from far below.

"I'm glad about it," Jack said. "Of course, I've always known that Alice loved you. That is why she wouldn't marry me. And I'm glad that when you are married in January you're going to take a long trip abroad. It will be good for both of you."

Mark's eyes were quiet now. His face was still thin, but color had been returning to it for over the past six months. He would never forget what had happened to him. But he would also never know the truth—if there was a "truth" involved.

"Of course," said Mark, "I'm not young any longer. I'm fourteen years older than Alice. But she doesn't seem to mind." He hesitated. "And she wants children."

"And you don't?"

Mark got up and began to walk slowly up and down the room. He had a fireplace in his apartment; he stopped to look at the fire. "I don't know," he said.

"Why not?"

Mark came back to his chair. He looked at Jack steadily. "I want the truth about something, Jack, and only you can tell me."

For an instant Jack was alarmed. And then he saw that

Mark's eyes were only troubled and uncertain, and not filled with horror. "Yes?" he said.

"There was Kathy and Alice is her sister," said Mark quietly. "You've told me all the traits of a psychopath. You've said they aren't inherited. But—Kathy. Well, she had some of the traits Angelo had. I've got to be frank, so that I'll know if it's safe to have—children. You see, Kathy didn't like people, either. She—and God forgive me for saying this about the poor girl—she was false to people, and often spiteful. She pretended to be interested in them, and sympathetic, and helpful, and anxious about their troubles. She wasn't, Jack. She—had mannerisms that deceived other people into thinking she was very kind and interested in them. She had a host of friends, who never caught on. Kathy—was greedy, like Angelo. And she was often malicious about people. Frankly, I never heard her say a good and sincerely kind thing about anyone. She would be all bubbles and radiance when we had guests; the door would hardly be shut on them when her face would change and she would talk meanly about all of them for hours. Jack, you understand? I loved Kathy. But I knew her. And I've been wondering—"

"You've been wondering if she wasn't a psychopath, too," said Jack, with pity. "Now let me ask you a few questions, Mark, and take your time and answer them openly and fully." He paused, and held Mark with his eyes.

"Think, now. Did Kathy love you?"

"Yes! I know she did. Without the slightest doubt."

"Did she love Alice?"

"Yes. She was jealous of her in some way, and I don't know why. But Alice lived with us after their parents died, and for years before Angelo was born. Kathy was seventeen years older than Alice; they were like a young mother and child together. Kathy would fuss over Alice like a mother; she was proud of her then, before Angelo came and took Alice's place in Kathy's emotions. She did her best for Alice; yes, she loved her. I think she never did stop loving her. She was as shocked as I was when Alice—almost dropped over the bluff that day." Even now, Mark could not say the awful words. "In fact, Kathy would have nightmares about it, and would wake up screaming, and I would have to reassure her that Alice was safe."

Jack nodded. "And her parents? Did she love them?"

"Very, very much. She was inconsolable for a long time after they died. I think she cared more for them than Alice did, but Alice was only a child then. Kathy nursed her mother during her last illness, and became sick over it."

Jack nodded again. "And Angelo. She really loved him, too?"

"Can you ask that?" Mark exclaimed. "She worshiped him."

"And none of all this expended love was false or insincere?"

"None," said Mark emphatically. "When it came to those she loved Kathy would have given her life, if necessary, for them."

He looked at Jack. "In fact, all of Kathy's life, misguided though it was sometimes, was all love."

Jack spread out his hands and smiled. "So, you see, Kathy was not a psychopath. The difference between a normal person and a psychopath is the ability to love others. Evil can't love anything but itself."

He stood up. "No matter how much we sin, if we love there is always forgiveness. But for evil, which cannot love, there is no redemption."